Copyright©2026 by Rise Above Books. No part of this book should be reproduced in any form, except for the inclusion of brief quotations in a review, without permission in writing from the author or publisher.

# THE TESTIMONY OF SILKY BLACK

## **Table of Contents**

Chapter 1: The Hatching

Chapter 2: Huddle Up

Chapter 3: Game Face

Chapter 4: Mandatory Uniform

Chapter 5: School is In

Chapter 6: Crown Me

Chapter 7: The Engine

Chapter 8: Motivation

Chapter 9: Turning Point

Chapter 10: The Second Half

## **Chapter 1: The Hatching**

It started again; Leon Townsend was daydreaming while staring into his bathroom mirror. He held a Gillette razor in his right hand. A deodorant product called axe and a bottle of 23 aftershave by Michael Jordan, sat on the counter near him. The fifty-two- year-old man was home alone; therefore, no one was around to bother him.

His hot tub was full of water waiting, for now it would just have to wait. He mentally reviewed his life, cherishing the good times and being thankful for overcoming the bad. The man's mind drifted back to high school days, while attending Phyllis Wheatley in Houston's Fifth Ward.

It was 1973, and Leon was fifteen years old. He was a fairly, good student; even though his female fan club did most of the work for him. His parents weren't too fortunate but still managed to keep clothes on their children. Leon was the youngest of three boys, with an older and younger sister.

"I appreciate your gift."

"You deserve it, Leon."

The halls were clearing out.

"I don't want to be late for class, so I'll catch you later."

The determined youngster hurried off. While rushing to class she mumbled, "Yes, yes, yes."

So far, her plan was working. While trotting to class himself, he thought about how he never mentioned his name, yet she spoke it well. The tardy bell rang right after he entered the door. Tralydia and Margie eyeballed him hard all throughout class.
The teacher was a recovering alcoholic hanging from a shaky limb.

Mr. Henry's class was considered rowdy compared to others; he didn't care. Tralydia gave the kid with rising popularity a piece of paper with her phone number on it after class. Margie watched closely. After Tralydia walked off, Margie stepped to him with an attitude.

Her brother was a spoiled brat that was given more clothes and valuables than he knew what to do with. That made it easy for her to take what she wanted. She didn't see it as stealing though. In her mind, it was just borrowing some stuff that her snobbish brother didn't need.

This same moment in time is when Ruthy began to do remarkable things with his clothes. Gradually, Ruthy's baby brother began to form a new image. Which in turn, highly impressed the onlooking admirers, even adding to their numbers. The once silent observers started speaking, some even sparked up casual conversation.

Leon jammed Shirley up as soon as he saw her again; exactly what she wanted. The growing teenager found her side, matching her pace as she walked down the hallway.

"What's up Shirley?"

"Nothing, just on my way to class."

They both slowed down a little.

While standing at his locker, he noticed the portly female entering his circumference. She stopped about three feet away. His facial expression said, "Who are you? And what do you want?"

Before he could say anything, she blurted out, "My name is Shirley." Her hand was extended for him to shake it. He shook it without introducing himself, not to be rude, just simply caught off guard. As soon as he released her hand, she shook her head as if snapping back to reality.

Then quickly said, "Here." She produced a full shopping bag held in her opposite hand. When the recipient accepted the bag, the girl walked off. With a quick glance it was obvious that the bag was full of clothes. The surprised new owner immediately dashed to the restroom to properly view them.

The bag contained three brand new shirts with matching pairs of pants. The tags were all intact. The Townsend kid wasn't used to having new clothes, so the tags were intentionally present when he wore them. Shirley already knew his name to say the least.

When one of them outgrew their vestment, it was required to give it to the next youngest. By the time the apparel made it to Leon, it would be rather worn. His older sister, Ruthy, couldn't stand to see her baby brother go to school looking like a bum.

Thus, she decided to garner his garments and put her creative touch to them. Earline didn't have to worry because Ruthy took good care of her things. Ruthy was a fabric freak that loved to sew and create little whatnots. Her half of the bedroom was filled with her creations. Earline even decorated her side with a few favorites.

Leon slept in the room with Eugene and Earl Jr. Earl Jr. was the oldest, not the smartest. Earl Senior worked at the waterfront; his wife Wilma worked as a maid for some well-off Black family across town. Their small three-bedroom house needed many repairs, gracefully it was still standing.

Earl's youngest son was jet black, tall, with good hair and perfect teeth. He noticed different girls watching him, but for some reason none would approach him. Whether it was coincidence or destiny something happened. A chubby, little chic approached Leon at school one day.

"Forget that b****! Let me write my number down for you."

Leon stood there, trying to contain his astonishment. She tore a piece of paper from her folder, jotted her home number down, then handed it to him. Both were considered a nice catch.

"Don't forget to call me ok."

Margie wagged her behind in a teasing manner as she strutted off. Leon stuffed the numbers in his pocket then headed on. Soon these scenes became common. Eugene witnessed much of it because he went to school with him. He told Earl Jr. and his sisters how the girls were acting behind Leon.

None were more excited than Ruthy. She was proud of him and happy to play a part in breaking the ice. At first, he hesitated to wear Ruthy's combination creations as she called them.

"Hell, nawgh Ruthy! I'm not wearing this!"

"Boy trust me, just trust me ok."

Her work became very noticeable via her new model. His hesitation suddenly transformed to anxiety. Even the teachers and other staff noticed the improvement in the lad's appearance. At home, Leon often found himself sitting near the old, withering peach tree in his tiny backyard.

It was fruitful at one time after his father planted it. Often, he pictured himself bearing fruit like the tree, never ever wanting to wither away. The small area near the woody perennial plant seemed to be his private thinking spot. His family would normally know exactly where to find him.

Basketball caught a lot of his attention. For years it was a favored pastime. The tall, brawny teen was good too. Most of his family possessed a little height. The basketball games always seemed to attract all types. You never knew who might show up at the park or some other neighborhood goal.

There was a man in his late twenties whose sobriquet was Mr. wonderful. He made special appearances at certain sporting events. The fly player drove a brand new, white convertible El Dorado Cadillac, with Superfly headlights and other custom accessories.

He flaunted a superb wardrobe, showy jewels, and a fleet of fine foxes. Leon wasn't naïve, he knew *what* Mr. Wonderful was doing. He just wanted to know *how* he was doing it. It wasn't odd for the fly guy to interest him; he was just one of many. Mr. Wonderful fascinated kids and grownups alike.

Ruthy's combination creations put a big dent in Shirley's plan. The determined kid refused to give up, so she plotted even harder. Her aim was to win her dream mate indecorously or however, by becoming well desired and indefeasible.

Being slightly overweight, she decided to kill two birds with one stone. Shirley compromised her normal meals and saved the money. Every two weeks the money saved was given to Leon. Patience helped endure the long-term process of her plan.

To her, his activities with other girls around the school were of little importance. Her reward would be much greater than a hard rod. She felt this deep inside of her heart and soul. Her family was more financially stable than his. She had every intention of using that to help bag him.

He continued to eat the bait that she was feeding too. She told herself, "I won't chase him, I just have to keep being patient." At the same time, Leon was becoming very accustomed to her polite treatment. Every now and then someone would slander her, but he wouldn't allow that.

One of his female admirers asked one day, "Why does that fat b**** always come around you?" He quickly responded, "Watch yo' mouth tramp!"
"Damn, it's like that?"
His reaction wasn't quite what she bargained for.

"Yea it's like that."

Shirley's future prize frowned at the girl, then walked off. It soon became known that Shirley was not to be disrespected. Basketball tryouts at school were near and Leon wanted to make the team.
The coaches knew about him before he even enrolled, which meant he was almost assured a position.

Eugene was already on the team, but this was his last year. He was an average player, and his younger brother would prove to be much better. Being on the team brought Eugene some attention that he wasn't getting. On a greater note, making the team and good performance would skyrocket Leon through the roof!

Shirley met him at his locker with her usual smile. "Good morning, Leon."

"Guess what Shirley!" His excitement was evident.

"What?"

"I made the team."

"That's good mister, I know you'll do well."

"I'm glad you feel that way."

His friend named Abdul walked up. Abdul was pro-Black and represented openly with much pride. "What's shaking my Black brother and sister?"

"I was just letting her know that I made the team."

"That's good news my brother."

Abdul stuck his hand out with the palm up, then excitedly shouted, "Lay it on me brother!" Leon happily gave him five, by slapping his hand. Then he stuck his hand out so Abdul could give him five. After giving each other five, they used the same hand to simultaneously stroke their afros to the back, laughing wildly.

Abdul emphasized, "Now that's what I'm talking about."

Shirley giggled at them, then waved while walking off.

"That chic really digs you man."

"It seems like it."

"If things really get rough, you'll find out for sure then."

Leon Townsend didn't have the slightest idea how rough things could be yet.

His coach told him, "Stop playing ball on the street because I don't want you to get hurt."

The new team member shook his head in agreement. "Okay Coach Hicks."

Coach Hicks used to play basketball and football too. He and his team were on a quest for their fourth state title in six years. Eugene warned his brother. "Coach Hicks is easy to get along with, but it ain't no jiving him. Just listen to him and don't goof off, and everything will be cool."

Practice was going well, everyone liked what they saw. Leon was instantly placed on the varsity team. News of the school's new player circulated around the schoolyard. More girls started to watch with wide eyes. The first game was approaching, and the onlookers wanted to see Leon perform.

At practice, his shooting percentage was high, not to mention he was slam-dunking left and right. At Shirley's house, there was a domestic dispute going on between her parents.

"I'm tired of you doing me like this Charles! It's not right!" Mrs. Lockhart was screaming, crying, and stomping her feet.

"Just listen damn it! I'm trying to explain to you."

"I'm not trying to hear it!"

She covered her ears and lost control. The frenzied woman began smashing his belongings and tossing them across the bedroom. Mr. Lockhart lunged at her, attempting to restrain her. She quickly weaved and zoomed through the door.

The distressed dame continued running through the front door to a neighbor's house. Charles Lockhart was in hot pursuit. Shirley ran to the front door, unsurprised by this reoccurring problem. She shook her head with disapproval, then went to examine the damage in her parents' bedroom.

She silently thought, "It's a mess." Her eyes rapidly focused on an opportunity. It was time for her to borrow something again. Silently she plotted, "Hmm, dad's jewelry box." It was turned over on the floor with jewelry everywhere. "Dad won't mind if I borrow a couple of rings."

She hastily grabbed two gold nugget rings and disappeared. "I'm glad my brother wasn't here. Leon will really like me when I give him these rings."

Mr. Lockhart banged on the neighbor's door across the street. For now, Gertrude was safe inside. Twenty minutes later, the local fuzz arrived. Mr. Lockhart hatefully cooperated with them. One of the officers strictly warned him. "If you hit her, you're going to jail."

The neighbors were tired of the noisy, unnecessary quarrels, but didn't want to turn their back on Gertrude. Before the cops left one of them advised, "I strongly suggest you two get marriage counseling." The Townsends were humble and nonchalant. They really didn't fight or fuss at all.

They were too busy trying to keep food on the table, and the bills paid. The kids knew of their hardships, so they tried to fend for themselves. Earl and Wilma did what they could when they could.

Leon's first game was against the Jack Yates Lions. He was playing power forward, making powerful moves, while the crowd cheered him on. Eugene was having a nice game too. Coach Hicks loved it along with the fans. Ruthy, Earline, and Earl Jr. rooted hard. Their parents couldn't make it but wished them well.

These teams were archrivals battling for more than a petty win. A few fights almost broke out, but the scuffles were quickly controlled. It was Third Ward against Fifth Ward, the crowd made that known. They yelled back and forth.

"Third Ward!"

"Fifth Ward!"

"Third Ward!"

"Fifth Ward!"

This was an annual thing for the two Black schools. They acted the same with every sporting event. The ongoing momentum kept the game interesting. Unfortunately for the Lions, they found out the hard way that the Wildcats had a new superstar.

He dunked consecutively and executed a high field percentage. The Wildcats were even wilder when the final buzzer went off. The cheerful home team danced and shouted, doing the robot, the funky chicken, and all kinds of stuff. The band rocked the house with the hyperactive crowd performing along with them.

The noisy event continued into the night, stemming small celebrations everywhere. Coach Hicks told Leon, "You were mighty nice boy, mighty nice." The coach patted him on the back while saying, "Keep up the good work Leon."

His siblings ran to greet him. They all hugged him at the same time. Their wonder caused them to overlook his dripping sweat. Shirley was hanging back a bit, waiting to be noticed by her hero. A few other fans and supporters greeted him as well.

In the mist of the heavy celebrating and thinning crowd, the new star heard a familiar voice. "Leon." In the direction of the voice stood Margie. She twisted her hips while moving towards him. He met her halfway into her stride. The young flame had on a short miniskirt, knee-high boots, and a revealing top.

Her makeup was starting to run from the heat and intensity of the game. Her afro puffs were neatly positioned; the costume jewelry accentuated her gear nicely. "You played good macho man."

"Thank you, cupcake."

"I'm your number one fan."

She gently rubbed his face while delivering her punchline. Margie wanted to leave him with that thought so she skated away. Shirley tried to contain her jealousy as she approached.

"Your fan club is really growing huh?" Her words were spoken softly, without attitude.

"I guess…so how did you like the game?"

"You were great, just like I said you'd be."

"Thank you, baby."

She knew he wanted to join the party, so she acted fast.

"Let me see your hand."

She reached for it as he offered it. The swift female slid one of the rings on his pinky finger. It was a perfect fit.

"Damn girl you be coming on wit it!"

"Yea, and every chic you mess with better come on wit it too. If not, they will answer to me. Enforce your rules, but don't lose your cool."

Shirley kissed him on the cheek, then demanded, "Go enjoy your friends and fans, but remember what I told you."

She walked off slowly, in full admiration of the teenage man that she was grooming. He slapped her on the butt while jogging by.

"Later baby."

She waved even though his back was facing her. The delighted athlete was puzzled at the way his real numero uno had flared up. She had never spoken like that before. Plus, the peck on the cheek was the first of any type of intimacy.

To himself he thought, "She saw Margie without a doubt. Which means Margie is going to give me something, or else. I like the sound of that."

Leon laughed to himself while joining the others. They noticed his new ring right away.

"Where did you get that ring?"

"Shirley gave it to me."

They all made crazy noises and remarks.

"Whaaatt?" "Oooohh!" "Say whaaattt?"

The Townsend family decided to head home and party by themselves. Earl Jr. pulled out a cheap bottle of wine. Everyone except Earline took turns drinking while they journeyed home. The walk wasn't considered short or long, but on nights like this fun. By the time they finally made it, they were buzzing.

They tried to keep a lid on Earline because she was only thirteen. She wasn't worried though, she'd get her chance. Once at home, everyone began to do their own thing. Leon posted up near the peach tree, remaining there awhile before concluding his night.

## Chapter Two: Huddle Up

Leon noticed the sudden change in his life, it felt good too. Everyone around him seemed to take notice. While at his most favorite thinking spot, he carefully evaluated the people and things that contributed to the sudden change, desiring to handle it all properly.

The hard thinker often viewed his life as a game of basketball, fast paced. The main objective was to win and keep winning. He vowed to never let things spin out of control; knowing that to maintain control it had to be exercised.

Everybody has a position to play; his job was to make sure they played it. That was the only way he could win. The Wildcats won their first game of the season, which was on a Friday. The following Monday fans were still excited. Margie stepped up to Leon at his locker.

She was close enough to smell the Dentyne chewing gum on his breath. The thinker had thought about what he would say to her over the weekend.

"Hey there macho man."

"What it is cupcake?"

"Why didn't you call me this weekend? I was looking forward to talking to you." She seductively aired.

"Check it out cupcake…" He paused, emphasizing seriousness. She took a step back because his body language demanded space.

"Are you just going to continue to be a fan, or are you going to play on my team?"

"What do you mean?"

"The only girls I mess with are the ones that do for me. So, if you wanna be on the team, I need some green."

Margie was shocked. "Boy who do you think you are? You must be crazy or something!"

She poked her lips out and wagged extra hard as she marched off. He didn't care; she was just one of many that was on his tip. He went on to class as usual. The smart girl that sat next to him leaned over and whispered, "I need to talk to you."

His body language told her to speak. Instead, she waited until after class.

"I'm sorry but I can't keep doing your work for you." She acted bashful with her head down, one foot playing with the other.

"Why?"

"It's just not right."

The adolescent walked off, knowing how it would be handled. The next day, the girl was cut off before entering the classroom.

"Look child, Leon is my man. If you don't keep doing his work, I'll work on you." Shirley's voice was calm but serious.

The frightened girl nervously nodded her head, signifying comprehension. That little problem and others like it were instantly handled. The tall youngster was growing fond of things becoming easier. Why would he ever want it to stop?

While walking down the hall a nice-looking student handed him a note. She was a pretty lamb that he had never seen before. It was intriguing how clothes and a smidgen of fame made such an enormous difference. The kid receiving popular demand would take full advantage. Eugene and Leon sat together in the cafeteria while eating lunch.

"I sure hope we keep winning."

The youngest brother gave a confident smile before responding. "We will, watch."

"Since this is my last year, I wanna go out in style." He spoke with a fly tone.

"Don't worry, as long as we're winning, I'm winning. If I have my way, I'm gonna flip this school upside down."

"I can dig it lil bro."

After basketball practice, Leon went home and called Shirley. On the way home he was solicited by an older, conspicuous loafer aimlessly wandering down the street. While in the process of passing him, the guy with bloodshot red eyes stopped him.

"Wanna buy some grass lil brother? It ain't homegrown either."

"I'll pass."

Nothing was abnormal about the incident; he didn't think twice about it. Once at home, his new shoes were removed to relax. They were purchased with funds given by Shirley. The rotary house phone was used to call her.

"Hello."

"What it be like baby?"

"Hello there you. I've been thinking about you as usual."

"Oh yea?"

"Boy don't play with me."

Despite her heart's desire, she knew having him to herself was farfetched. Seeing this as reality, she encouraged him to explore and expand, without leaving her out of course. Someone taught her well, because she knew that trying to prevent an eagle from soaring would only leave her in the wind.

"I see great things in your future homeboy, and I definitely plan to be a part of it."

"You're already a part of it. Just stay down and stick around baby."

"I'm going to help you as much as I can, and it's all my pleasure."

The devoted teen exhaled hard, stuck in the middle of a beautiful fantasy. The two chitchatted for a few minutes then disengaged. So far, the helpful admirer was simpatico. Wilma Townsend acknowledged her son's first win. Her job caused her to be absent a lot, so this was the first chance to see him since the game.

"Congratulations on your game Leon." She sounded somewhat enthused.

"Thank you, Mama. We're gonna win the next one too. Hopefully you can come watch me play one day."

"I hope so too son, maybe one day I'll surprise you."

He didn't bother mentioning something like this to his father because he always seemed uninterested. Although his parents never argued, Earl Sr. didn't appear to be happy. His kids wondered why he even stuck around. None of them dared question his authority or personal business though.

They didn't have the guts to do that.
His offspring witnessed and experienced his fury over the years. The industrious man was normally settled, but if riled he could easily turn into a monster.
His attitude and personality reminded the kids of James on the show Good Times.

As they matured, they realized the family needed him. Earl Jr.'s girlfriend walked into Ruthy's room while she was hard at work.

"What chu doing girl?"

"I'm fixing up some of Leon's clothes."

"Let me see girl. I know he's a fly cat. Those girls at his school must be going crazy."

Ruthy was eighteen, Earl Jr. and his girl were both nineteen. Eugene was seventeen with a jail record already. Fortunately, it didn't affect his school activities. Leon was busy plotting to pay his personal tailor that worked so hard for him.

The thinker wanted to reward key players on his team, certainly her if nobody else. In addition, it would be incentive for them to work harder.
People began to see hunger and ambition in this teenager's eyes.

The next game was only a couple of days away; everyone was looking forward to it. Coach Hicks rubbed his sideburns, signals for certain plays. Abdul waited around school until Leon was through practicing. They often walked home together.

"I gotta hurry up and get home, so I can catch this Jesse Jackson speech on tv."

"Man, I'm tired. You can go ahead I'll check you later."

"I'm not sweating it, he'll be there."

Abdul wanted to learn more about his people. The next day, Adbul greeted him with his power fist raised.

"Power to the people!"

Leon playfully snickered then uttered, "Power to the people!" He regained seriousness and asked, "Did you learn something yesterday?"

"I sure did."

"What did you learn?"

"That I shouldn't have waited on yo' a**!"

"Awgh s***!"

They laughed for a while.

It was game day again, and all were restless. The Colts from Evan E. Worthing were the present opponents. They played at the Leroy Livingston gymnasium. Eugene and Leon said their final words to Abdul and Shirley before grouping with the team.

Abdul hurled out, "Power to the people!"

Eugene launched out, "Right on brother!"

The hyper twosome gave each other five.
Eugene added, "Now on the backside." Once they concluded their joyous handshake, Abdul stuck his hand out to Leon.

"Gimme me some skin boy!"

Leon abruptly complied, hugged Shirley, then jogged off to the rest of the team. Eugene followed. Before reaching the boys, the jog became a slow walk. One of the cheerleader captains, Princess, intentionally rubbed his arm when he walked by. She reacted astoundingly.

"Damn...you silky...Black."

Princess quickly covered her gaping mouth, without even realizing what she was doing.

The opening minutes were upon them. When the players took the court the Wildcat cheerleaders went into action. Their new cheer took everyone by surprise.

"Silky Black! Sil...ky Black! Silky Black! Sil...ky Black!"

They were cheering and raving hard in their purple and white uniforms. Initially, the whole gym was unaware of who Silky Black was. Before the game ended everyone knew exactly who he was.
The Townsend brothers and their team gave the onlookers a good show.

Ruthy and Earl Jr.'s mate, Charlotte, walked in near the end of the first quarter. Leon performed with fancy footwork and effective scoring maneuvers. Coach Hicks silently began to grant, "This boy was born to play."

Every time he scored the cheerleaders chanted. "Silky black! Sil...ky Black!" The new nickname caught on like a wild forest fire. The Colts were leading by four points at halftime. It was a close game all the way through. The crowd was on their feet most of the final minutes.

Both sides were on edge with their fingers crossed, with back-to-back baskets scored. In the closing moments, Silky Black landed an amazing three pointer that won the game. "Whoosh" was the sound made from the nets. The Wildcat fans jumped for joy, yelled, celebrated! It filled the place with glee, minus the losing crowd.

The female students at Worthing had something new to talk about now, they knew him as Silky Black. The word started to spread that Wheatley had a serious threat. After the game, big sis had to do some investigation.

"Boy where did this Silky Black stuff come from?" She asked as if the new moniker was a little off base.

Still breathing hard, he answered while wiping sweat from his face. "One of those cheerleaders rubbed on me and went crazy." His answer was presented jokingly, yet he was dead serious. Charlotte stood there, soaking it all up.

"If you say so Mr. Silky Black." Ruthy was moved by the surname, so was the owner of it.

Eugene strolled over towards his relatives. They made him feel good about his performance also. The high school senior couldn't wait to puff on his fat party joint, soon the cannabis cigarette would be smoking in his mouth.

Silky Black's eyes searched for Shirley, but she was gone. He phoned her at home.

"Why did you leave?" Disappointment surfaced in his voice.

"You didn't need me, did you?"

"That's beside the point."

"You never asked me to stay."

"You're right, but still…Did you see the entire game?"

"I saw it all, Silky Black. Your game winning shot was the coolest."

"I was so glad I didn't miss."

In the back of his mind, it was a piece of cake as he highly anticipated the next game.

Ruthy conjured up a surprise for the next game. She walked in with a poster board that read, "Go Silky Black!" Charlotte accompanied her with one that read, "Silky Black on the attack!" The warm sister really supported her little brother.

He started the game off with a film worthy slam! The team quickly built a large lead that they held throughout the game. The Wheatley Wildcats were now 3-0. The following week, more posters were seen in the crowd bearing the new star's name.

Ruthy, Charlotte, and Shirley had on t-shirts with Silky Black in glitter on the front side. The supportive sister made them herself of course. Coach Hick's team snagged another victory, improving their record to 4-0. After the contest, Leon was approached by a female in bell bottoms and a tie-around top.

She handed him four five-dollar bills. The agile youngster shoved the money into one of his socks.

Then asked, "What made you change your mind?"

"Because you're Silky Black."

Margie's answer pleased him yet left an uncertain taste in his mouth. The novice mack felt like giving her an order.

"Don't let it take this long next time."

"But I don't know what to do." The confused girl admitted.

      Regretfully, he didn't either. Nonetheless, admitting that would certainly sink his game. The thinker had to think fast.

"Look, don't hold out on me ok! You bring me some more money, then I'll take you to get even more."

      The tired player was trying to stall while coming up with a plan. The hot hoochie wandered off, in search of the thing that would please her desired one. The most ironic thing happened next.
Mr. Wonderful made his way toward Leon.

      He saw the fabulous man headed his way, wondering if he was coming to talk to him.

"That was a good game you played today youngster."

"Thank you."

"I'm Mr. Wonderful."

The well-dressed street king attempted to shake Leon's hand. The young hooper hastily wiped his hand on his shorts, then shook the legend's hand.

"My real name is Leon, but now they call me Silky Black."

"Right on, I can dig it. I used to see you at the park sometimes. The coach told you to stay away, I concluded."

"He doesn't want me to get hurt." It was spoken as if the coach was overprotective.

"That's good though youngblood, listen to him because he knows the deal."

"Mr. Wonderful, can I ask you something?"
The inquirer couldn't pass up this opportunity.

"You wanna know how to get money out of that sexy lil number you were just rapping with don't cha?"

"That's right." The hooper tried to contain his amazement. He pulled twenty dollars out of his sock. "She just gave me this, but I need somewhere to take her." He started to mention Shirley, however, chose not to put all his cards on the table.

"How old are you youngblood?" The young upcoming mack interested him.

"Fifteen."

"Fifteen huh?"

Leon nodded his head. The man with the small, dark brown afro and light mustache, pondered for a moment. "The kid seems to have plenty of potential. Basketball is going good for him. I wouldn't mind giving him a little game."

The pander spoke again. "Check this out, call me tomorrow and I'll come pick you up." A business card was handed to him, as he walked off.

Leon, now known as Silky Black, was in utter disbelief. "A street legend actually walked up and introduced himself to me." The game was beginning to suck him in fast. Eugene crept up with wide eyes.

"That was Mr. Wonderful you just got through talking to."

"I know." The response was nonchalant.

The glitter girls turned some heads, which gave him an idea. The small crew piled in Charlotte's mother's Volkswagen bug. They were stuffed like sardines. Eugene was musty, making the ride more unpleasant.

Charlotte was driving the small car awaiting the pull from the musty boy's cigarette. She dropped him off first, a silently unanimous decision. The tall, brown-skinned senior got dropped off at his ex-girlfriend's cousin's house. It was all about convenience for him.

Earl Jr. felt totally different about his flame though. He considered the relationship with Charlotte to be infallible.

Leon and Ruthy were the darkest kids in the family. They were the only ones whose name didn't start with an E. It was never mentioned among them, yet there was a blur locked away in the back of their subconscious minds.

Could it be this subconscious blur that contributed to their drive and incentive? They felt compelled to succeed against all odds. Earl Sr. was a dark-skinned man that never smiled. His wife was an overworked, brown-skinned woman aging fast.

Charlotte pulled up at Abdul's house next. The struggling student jumped out, faced them, then waved. "Later y'all."

They all commented. "Later." "Bye Abdul." "Bye boy." Shirley rode with her brother. The orange bug headed to the Townsend residence. The thinker couldn't contain his present thoughts; he wanted to see their reactions anyway.

"I plan to have some real money pretty soon. You know I'm gonna take care of you, big sis."

"What chu got cooking now boy?" Ruthy was interested.

"I'm gonna get some girls and get paid. You'll see big sis."

"Are you talking about what I think you're talking about?"

"Yep, and I'm dead serious."

Charlotte looked in the rearview mirror and smiled at him, admiring his confidence. He had plans for them too but wasn't ready to inform them. A few more things needed to fall in place first. Wilma was at home for a change when the kids came in.
The mother of five had cooked an adequate soul food meal for the family.

The contents of the pots were still hot; the aroma reached the other side of the front door.
The arriving group rushed to the bathroom to wash their hands.

"That food smells so good." Charlotte licked her lips while rinsing her knuckles.

"Hell yea." Leon agreed.

"Hurry up girl." Ruthy playfully pushed her, her stomach told her to.

    Wilma started fixing plates for the trio, knowing the grand rush was on. Earl Sr. ate before he left, the other kids had just finished. The feared father went to meet friends at a local blues club. He was a diehard B.B. King and Johnny Taylor fan.

    Wilma set the table, placing the plates with generous servings on it. The hungry bunch were already seated when the plates arrived. The smacking teens devoured the neckbones, turnip greens, pinto beans, and homemade cornbread.

    Leon rubbed his tummy then blurted out, "Thank you Mama." A loud belch followed.

## Chapter 3: Game Face

The next day, anxiety was eating Silky Black up. As soon as he got home from school, Mr. Wonderful's number was dialed. The car phone rang in his plush Cadillac.

"Hello."

"May I speak to Mr. Wonderful please."

The man recognized the voice right away.
"Silky Black, what a pleasure. Are you ready to roll with the best?"

He quickly responded. "Is a pig fat like a smart cat?"

"Right on, right on." His response amused the older vet. "Okay well meet me at the store on Lockwood and Market in about thirty minutes."

"I'll be there."

The yearning youth wiped his ring and shoes off, brushed his teeth and hair again, then headed out.

He took his time walking to the nearby store. At the designated meeting point, he observed two schoolmates fighting. A small crowd of teenagers were spectating the brawl.

"Get'em! Get'em!"

"Don't let that fool do you like that!"

"Punch his lights out!"

"You can do it, you can do it, come on!"

    Neither one of them were friends of his, so he didn't care to entertain the juvenile disruption. His mind was on having big money anyway. That's why he stood at a distance, refusing to be affiliated with their mess.

    The angry store owner barged through the door with a large, long steel object resembling a bat. The furious Asian man waved the weapon at the wild bunch while shouting.

"Get away from here! Go home to your parents." The Oriental accent was heavy. The aggravated pack yelled and threw rocks as they abandoned the scene.

"F*** you old man!"

"Go back to China Ching Ching!"

The store owner wasn't even Chinese, they didn't know, nor did they care. The youngsters continued verbalizing threats and racial slurs as they left. The livid merchant returned to the safety of his small storefront.

The plausible onlooker decided to patronize with the man, by buying some gum. This was done so he could be distinguished from the troublemakers. The disruptive school kids weren't on his level, soon that fact would be known to everyone.

Silky Black used courtesy everywhere he went. When the man handed him his change, a pleasing moment arose.

"Thank you, have a nice day."

"You too." The reply came with a smile.

    A beautiful white caddy pulled up moments after Leon exited the door. It was Mr. Wonderful without a doubt. When the car parked, the driver gestured, signaling for him to approach. A sexy female opened the passenger door and stepped out.

    She was a chocolate-skinned babe with shoulder length braids. A short, skintight sequined dress held the sculptured curves of her soft frame. Her lips were glossy, eyes hazel, and her ears possessed big loop earrings made of gold. Gogo boots enclosed her feet and calves.

    Silky viewed the gorgeous doll from head to toe, appreciating her beauty and taking notes. She lifted the passenger seat up, allowing him to sit in the back. Once inside, he had officially entered Mr. Wonderful's world. It felt good too.

The woman's soft voice was aired. "Are you all the way in?"

She was referring to his feet so she could close the door. However, the question meant much more to the fifteen-year-old known as Silky Black. He took a deep breath, exhaled, then answered.

"Yes, thank you."

His manners helped the woman see some of what her besieger saw in him. The car held a very pleasing fragrance. For a long moment he almost thought it was a dream. He had too much pride to pinch himself.

"Could it be? It really is a peach smell. It's definitely meant for me to be here."

Mr. Wonderful kept peach car freshener in reach. The car went in reverse once the door was closed. The new passenger leaned back to enjoy the comfort of the luxury vehicle. The driver extended his hand towards the relaxed passenger as he spoke.

"This is Brown Sugar; she sure is sweet too."

The backseat guest silently agreed.

"Brown Sugar, this is Mr. Silky Black."

"I'm pleased to meet you Mr. Silky Black."

She turned around and gave a polite smile.

"The feeling is mutual."

The respect factor made everyone feel good, especially the young mack. It highly pleased him to be in the company of such a man, and to be respected as a man. Once the car was moving a different type of atmosphere seemed to engulf the Townsend's youngest son.

The sweet smell of success was all around him. He rejoiced while consuming as much of the available air as possible. The volume on the eight-track increased as Earth, Wind, and Fire came through the speakers.

Heads were bobbing and fingers were snapping. While still in Fifth Ward, they pulled up at the corner of Florida and Jensen Drive. Brown Sugar knew the routine. She pecked Mr. Wonderful on the cheek, then hopped out. The polite prostitute lifted the seat up, then Silky claimed it.

"I'll do my best as usual daddy."

The chocolate working girl scurried away to occupy her position. The boss pulled off in route to a local pool hall.

"That's one of my main girls right there. She's been with me for about four or five years. Can you dig it?"

"Yea I can dig it."

Mr. Black couldn't hold his question any longer.

"What makes you dig the peach smell?"

"I like sweet stuff man you know, sweet money, sweet women, sweet cars, sweet clothes, sweet smells, and sweet living. It ain't nothing sweeter than a peach or honey man."

"That's live stuff. I have an old peach tree in my backyard where I sit and think."

"No jive? Well, you're headed in the right direction then young mack."

    The guider of the dream car stuck his hand out, then his passenger gave him five. The air conditioner was very soothing, adding to the smoothness of the ride.

"Listen close, I don't want you to miss nothing. When I was coming up in this game, I had to learn most of this on my own. Nobody really taught me nothing. And you know what, I made many costly mistakes."

    There was a brief hesitation as they stopped at a red light.

"As you can tell, I eventually got my s*** together. However, I went through a hell of a lot first. You on the other hand, have a major advantage. Do you know what that advantage is?"

The high school student didn't want to give a dumb answer, which made him say,

"Tell me."

The driver discreetly laughed a little, flattering himself. "Why of course, me." The seriousness was maintained again. "As long as you respect the game, I'll school you."

The car was on the move again.

"If I bring you into the brotherhood, it's very important that you listen to me. If you screw up a lot will fall on me. Do you understand Mr. Silky Black?"

"I'm with you so far." The teen sounded confident.

"Good, now we can proceed. You gotta get yo' girls ready for the track. That's where it all happens at Jack. Yo' game must be really strong to compete with the older players. Yo' stable can't be weak either. I have a real good feeling about you though. Otherwise, you wouldn't be with me."

The mentor decided to let that sink in for a while. His new pupil thought silently to himself. The teacher wanted to advance him straight into the big league. The look on the passenger's face indicated serious thought.

That's exactly what it would take, along with courage and dedication. Earning respect from the big boys wasn't going to be easy. Fortunately, a major plus was in his corner. By the time Silky Black finished growing, he reached 6'4. Presently he was sizable for his age.

That fact along with his demeanor made him appear older. Soon his actions would certainly demarcate him from the rest. The driver began to speak again while they were coasting.

"We gonna swing by this lil joint where a few of the players hang out. You need to know each other."

Things seemed to be moving fast for the blossoming virile. Shortly after informing the attentive passenger of their destination, they arrived.

"Come on in."

The driver made the request while exiting the vehicle. He stepped out with a shiny, impressive suit that made him favor a popular singer that ruled the airwaves. The fabulous outfit twinkled along with his massive diamonds. His presidential Rolex and big rings had ice all over them, freshly glazed alligators decorated his feet.

Point blank, the dude was super sharp. While looking at him, Silky Black said to himself, "I can't wait to step my game up."

Mr. Wonderful opened the door to the modest pool hall, then entered. His new protégé tailed him at a respectable distance. They both stood about six feet, yet the basketball favorite was still growing. The elite group greeted them.

"Hey Mr. Wonderful, what it be like?"

Everyone gave him five. Silky lifted his head to them while standing back, which was a form of speaking. Mr. Wonderful beckoned Silky to come forth. Once he stood at a formidable position, the introductions began.

"This is Silky Black y'all. Silky Black this is Easy Money Sunny, Pink Paradise, Luscious Larry, Too Cool Ken, and King Paul."

He shook hands with each one as they were introduced, all were spruce.

Too Cool Ken announced, "You cool with Mr. Wonderful, you cool with us."

The newcomer spoke for the first time. "I appreciate that."

While staring into his small pocket mirror, Luscious Larry stated, "It's nothing but love here baby." Larry stayed in the mirror more than his women; it didn't matter his ladies were stuck on him too. Silky followed his tutor's lead and stepped towards the bar.

They sat on the leather stools for a few minutes. A scrawny beldam with heavy breasts walked towards them from the other side of the bar.

"Hello Mr. Wonderful, how are you?" She was always thrilled to see him.

"I'm fine Mrs. Renee, thank you."

They traded happy faces with one another. A lilt by Kool and the Gang was playing in the background. Before he had a chance to introduce him, the retired hooker curiously asked,

"Who's your friend?"

"I'm Silky Black Mam." The apprentice saved the older player's breath.

The young lad shook her hand.

"Call me Mrs. Renee." The retired vet winked her eye at the fast learner. "So, what are we drinking gentlemen?" She laid both hands on the bar, insinuating that her attention was solely on them.

"Scotch on the rocks, and whatever he wants."

"Nawgh, I'm cool thanks anyway."

Mrs. Renee could schmooze the best of them.

"Are you sure honey?" There was an acute do it for me look on her face. The new guest reconsidered.

"I'll take a virgin drink."

"Thank you honey." She was pleased.

Mr. Wonderful patted his friend on the back.

"You catch on fast lil bro. A true player never sits at the bar without buying a drink, even if he doesn't drink it."

His eyes showed comprehension. Mrs. Renee served them immediately. The three of them small talked a few minutes. A shallow crowd gave her a chance to join in. Pink Paradise moseyed on over to the bar.

"Give me my usual."

"Ok Pinky."

In a split second, the fresh glass of pink passion was in the pink lover's pink palm. The flamboyant male was infatuated with pink; some even thought it was a mental illness of some sort. Any item that he owned that could be pink was indeed pink.

He had a pink house inside and out, pink cars, pink wardrobe, unbelievable amounts of pink whatnots, and flaunted jewelry with an amazing abundance of pink sapphires. The only thing accepted not being pink was money.

The pink happy man was nowhere near sweet, putting plenty of chumps in check. He was no stranger to danger and would whoop a** or shoot a clown in a heartbeat!

He became a well-known and well-respected mack across the country. The word on the street was, "Don't try the pimp in the pink!" Pink Paradise sipped his rose' while socializing with other members of their subculture. Several chicks mingled about while pool, card, and dice games were being played.

Mr. Wonderful told his passenger, "I'll be right back." He went to pull Easy Money Sonny's coat about a foul situation. In an instant, a lewd jade sat on a stool next to him. She was a sneaky renegade named Prasilla. The wild rebel quickly tried to test his integrity.

"You look kinda young, boy you better get out of here."

He calmly replied, "The name is Silky Black."

"Silky who?" Prasilla tried to be funny. When she noticed his perfect white teeth, it appealed to her, but she would never admit it.

The young man didn't appreciate her trying to downplay him at all. He swiftly made it clear.

"Look, if you're not trying to pay me, at least pay attention."

The comment hit her hard. She angrily groaned then blurted, "Young cat you ain't ready yet!"
She made an ugly face before tramping off.
Mr. Wonderful saw the quick episode from across the room. A couple of minutes later, he returned.

"Come on let's split."

Mrs. Renee waved as they left.

"See you later Mrs. Renee."

The clean caddy was occupied again.

The driver said, "One more stop, then I'll take you home."

"That's cool."

The good soul music kept flowing.

"I like the way you handled that outlaw broad. Whatever you said to that no-good tramp had her steamed up. Tramps like her need to stay mad, because all they do is take up space for a good hoe. When they get down and out, they try to run to a pimp for help. When in reality, they really don't like us."

The person seated next to him was listening like never before.

"If a chic like that ever chooses you, don't give her nothing, and treat her like a dog. Catch my drift?"

Prasilla's attitude really made him shake his head in agreement.

"I would have to dog a chic like that."

"Right on lil bro."

The two ended up on O.S.T. and Scott, on the South side of town at the World Fair. Customers came from far and near to shop at this popular center. They didn't stay long because he wanted to get Leon home at a fairly, decent time. The convertible pulled up at the Townsend home at about eight-thirty.

"Call me tomorrow lil bro."

"Cool, later."

The driver pulled off while the passenger neared the front door. The tutor purchased four suits and a pair of ostrich shoes for the upcoming mack. The excited teen had never worn a suit or expensive shoes before but couldn't wait to wear them now.

Leon darted straight into his room to further appreciate his gifts; privacy was out of the question though. That was ok for now, he wasn't trying to hide his new vines. While in their bedroom, the brothers fired away.

"Where did you get this stuff? How much did it cost?"

"Who took you? What made you want suits?"

The questions kept coming and coming.
He remembered exactly what to tell them.

"The game bought this for me."

"The game?"

  The older brothers were puzzled. They didn't want to seem stupid, so it was left alone. It was time to go to his favorite spot. He hugged Ruthy and kissed Earline on the way outside. Earl Sr. was in his room sleeping while Wilma was at work.

  Leon sat on the stump near the aging peach tree. He slowly reviewed the entire day before planning for the next. Mr. Wonderful's words replayed in his head. "The track is where it's at Jack!" Brown Sugar was eager to work it too.

"I need girls like that. I also need to learn the track. Learn the track...."

Learning the track was number one on his list. The older players were mentally analyzed. He thought about Pink Paradise in his hot pink suit, with his obvious degree in pinkology.

Luscious Larry had a Shirley Temple perm with crinkled curls falling everywhere, and a smile displaying a couple of gold teeth. Too Cool Ken was a short, baby face brother with long fingernails and cornrows. They considered him a yellow fellow because of his bright skin.

King Paul was a fat mack that made being fat seem cool. He was the most exuberate stout man Silky Black had ever seen. Easy Money Sonny had a neatly trimmed full beard with a bald head. He was masculine and very mean-looking, having the build of a wrestler or heavyweight boxer.

They all seemed pretty cool. One thing was for certain; they were all about money. Their styles were so much different from each other, yet similar qualities, purpose, and beliefs brought these individuals together.

"Shirley will be put to the test real soon, as well as others."

The teen collected a few more thoughts before going inside. A stray cat that Earline had been feeding crossed his path.

"Meow...meow..."

"If you're smart, you'll get fat."

The hungry cat trotted behind him.
Leon slammed the door on the deprived animal.
The feline sat at the door for a while before giving up.

"Meow, meow, meow."

The fuzzy stray strayed away after the unsuccessful attempt. If Earline had been aware of the kitten's presence, she would have scraped up something for her feline friend. The Townsends were winding down for the night. Those that weren't already asleep were on their way. The youngest boy eventually got some rest.

## Chapter 4: Mandatory Uniform

The next morning, the new suit owner could not wait to put one on. Therefore, the bathtub was quickly used. He brushed and flossed his Hollywood teeth before bathing. The bathroom mirror began to reflect a Colgate smile. Deodorant was placed under his armpits after drying off. Johnson's baby powder fell on his feet, chest, and groin area.

Eugene banged on the door.

"Hurry up boy! You ain't the only one that need to use it."

Leon slung the hollow door open then sarcastically uttered, "Boo." He rudely shoved past in route to the bedroom. Eugene frowned but overlooked him while entering the restroom.

Ruthy was up early too preparing to go job hunting. She noticed that the Ford pickup wasn't in the driveway, which meant her father was already gone to work. The crafty young woman helped her sister get ready for school.

Ruthy had an average build for a young woman, with a peculiar face. Her creative combinations attracted more attention from guys. Females began to adore her creativity too, which gradually started to put change in her pocket.

Earline was developing fast but was only thirteen. Ruthy touched up Earline's pigtail before tending to her own matters. She aided all her siblings focusing on the youngest two. They all managed to show appreciation in their own ways.

Unlike some families, they all got along. A horn blew outside. "Beep beep." It was Charlotte waiting on Earl Jr. to come outside. She took him to work when possible; he worked part-time selling papers for the Houston Post. Usually, the oldest brother was relaxed, when Charlotte came around, he became rather jolly.

Anyone could see that his nose was wide open for her. Earl Jr. was nothing like Leon because Charlotte kept him broke. The two younger brothers shook their heads at Earl Jr. They discovered that talking to him was useless.

She wasn't happy unless he was giving her money or kissing her butt. One day Eugene suggested, "Somebody else probably laying your woman more than you." That comment almost started a fight. Thankfully, Leon was there to break it up. The statement affected him because deep down inside it was probably true.

The whimpering wimp had to beg for sexual relations. The dominatrix even slapped him around when they were alone, her little puppy was trained. He was able to have others but was sprung. He almost tripped over his tongue at first sight.

The searching shark knew she had him right away. The juicer always managed to keep at least one sucker at her disposal. The gamer played her cards right around his siblings and close friends. The undercover pill-head popped a tree early that morning before driving to get Earl Jr.

He knew about her secret habit, assuming no one else did. The jolly sap sprinted out the door and into the orange bug. The driver seemed a tad bit jumpy.

He asked, "What's wrong with you? You on that stuff early this morning?"

Her eyes and facial expression were a dead giveaway. He knew the answer already, still waiting for a response.

"Boy shut up and leave me alone."

She spoke with a calm influence from the drug. The car went in reverse. Her gullible boyfriend's face held a smirk for quite some time, howbeit nothing else was mentioned about it. She was in a daze while driving, her countenance was a deadpan. Earl Jr. was upset but spoke calmly.

"Look at you. You look like a zombie."

She dumbfoundedly muttered, "Huh?" Then she managed to mumble, "I told you to leave me alone." Her voice was low and sluggish.

A part of him was glad when he made it to work. Nevertheless, he feared for her safety while driving home. The paperboy kissed his main squeeze, then pinned her to the seat by her shoulders.

Next, he aggressively shook her in hopes of sobering her up. It was either that or multiple slaps. Eventually the slaps would be returned, so the shaking method was chosen. The driver shook her head and rubbed her face. Charlotte slowly came back to life.

"Gone on boy, I'm alright."

His woman was much more alert, voice still dragging. Finally, he was confident enough to let her go. She blew him a kiss while pulling off. He silently prayed for her before entering the workplace.

Sometimes someone would walk Earline to school. Since becoming a little older, the blossoming teen strolled on her own more. This particular morning, she caught a ride with a neighbor.
The young girl pranced down the street and hopped in the car with her friend Yolunda. Yolunda's parents drove an old, beat-up dodge but it was dependable.

The preponderant brother yelled to the restroom. "Do you want me to wait on you?"

Eugene answered, "It's up to you."

Silky Black smiled from ear to ear when he placed his new suit on. The exotic ostrich shoes topped it off. He happily joked, "Mirror mirror on the wall, I know I'm the cleanest young mack of all." He brushed his thick, wavy hair while admiring himself.

While waiting on Eugene to finish getting dressed, Leon appeared at Ruthy's threshold.

"Check out the new threads big sis."

He held his arms outward which was a form of profiling. Her head lifted with astonishment.

"Ooh…look at my lil brother."

She instantly leaped to give a firsthand inspection. Hand-me-downs were becoming scarce in his wardrobe. The self-made fashion designer examined him from head to toe.

"You are sharp as a tack boy."

Her hands still maneuvered along his clothing, as he modestly spun around for her. She stepped back with folded arms still staring at him, then said, "Whatever you got going make sure you keep it up."

"Do you think you can make some clothes like these?"

She thought briefly, "I can try my best."

"I believe in you, big sis, more than you know."

He turned and walked back to his bedroom, leaving the thought to settle in her mind.
Eugene announced, "I'm ready." He took a good look at his brother then proclaimed, "You must be running for president or something, because you clean as can be."

The suit was peach with tan detail. Tan socks, shirt, tie, and ostrich shoes completed the outfit. Eugene thrust out, "Too bad we're walking." Leon just grinned. When they stepped through the front door, Eugene noticed Charlotte sitting patiently in the driveway.

The peach freak shared, "That's our ride right there." The effects of the pill were gradually wearing off. She leaned over to unlock the door upon noticing them. They jumped in and closed the door, then the car was put in motion. The small car rolled towards Wheatley High School with soothing soul on the radio.

The early morning tunes gave them more energy to burn throughout the day. The well-dressed young man anticipated an extraordinary day, certainly planning to get the most out of it. When the vehicle reached the school, Leon climbed out feeling refreshed.

The luxuriant youth aimed to complete his mission. Once Eugene was clear of harm, Charlotte smashed off. Silky tapped his brother in the chest, seeking his attention.

"Remember what I told you about turning this school upside down?"

"I'm hip."

"Well, it's already starting to tilt."

"Lay it on me lil bro!"

They gave each other five while treading onto the campus. The Townsend kid was dressed better than all the teachers and the staff. When Abdul saw him, he joked,

"I heard we were up for a new dean, but I didn't know it was you." They slapped hands as usual.

"I'm just trying to show these chicks how a real mack is supposed to look. Once they start keeping me paid, I can look like this every day. Ya dig?"

"Stay on top of it then powerful Black man."

Shirley quietly walked up. "What's shaking you two? I'm not blind, so I see it's definitely you."
The admirer's lips abruptly found his jaw.
"I couldn't help myself, I'm sorry."

"Never be sorry baby, sorry has no place with me."

Abdul drifted off so they could have a moment. His appearance apparently cluttered her thoughts.

"Well, I'm...I mean...awgh forget it.
You understand, don't you?" She tried to erase the frustration from her face.

"It's cool baby, everything will be alright."

His right hand gently lifted her chin. Shirley sighed hard, expressing relief.

"So how do I look baby?"

"Silky Black, you look marvelous." Her face lit up like a light bulb while complimenting him.

"Thank you, sweet baby."

"I'm only telling the truth."

"This is only the beginning, and I need you to keep this going."

"What else can I do?"

"I need you to work the track for me."

"The track?"

Her face held a confusing frown. She knew what the track was, but that was it. At the time, he didn't know much more than her; yet swore to change that overnight. He wanted to have her out there in less than a week.

"Yea baby, that's where the cabbage is. We can make many things happen like that. Don't you want me to have a car and other nice stuff?"

"You know I do; you don't have to ask me that."

"Well, I'm telling you what we need to do."

"That reminds me, I have something for you." Shirley dug in her purse and pulled out the other ring. "Here." It was handed to him with a smile.

"You're a bad mamma jammer Shirley."

The ring was placed on the middle finger of his right hand. The trivial things were gradually beginning to add up.

"I don't want to be too late for class."

"I can dig it."

The girl speedily ambled away with her head spinning. He bumped into Margie next. Her eyes almost popped out of her head when she saw him.

"Wow! You look good."

"I try cupcake. What about you, have you been trying?" His slick question caught her off guard.

The teenager with the body of a young woman, broke down because she didn't have any money. She grabbed her face with both hands in embarrassment.

"Silky Black I'm sorry but I don't have any dough."

"Sorry, sorry…" His volume increased.
"Everybody wanna be sorry for some strange reason. I don't have time for sorry Margie."

"What do you want me to do?" The fledgling tried not to sob.

"I want you to do what I tell you, that's what.
It's simple Margie, just bring me something to let me know that you trying. Then we can go to the next stage." His voice had lowered while maintaining the same seriousness. "Don't try to pull my leg either."

"I'm not, I swear I'm not." She knew he was serious without a doubt.

"Well, what are you waiting on?"

"Ok, ok."

She departed with a craving to fulfill Silky Black's wishes. He knew how she needed to be handled because her actions and attitude favored Prasilla. It wouldn't be surprising if they were related. The halls were almost completely empty when one of his teammates stopped him.

"Man, you running for mayor or something?"

"Something like that."

"What happened to you yesterday?"

It suddenly dawned on the rising star that he missed practice. He tried to answer swiftly.

"I had some business to take care of."

"Looks like you're taking care of some business today too."

"Yea I am. I might not be able to come today either."

The track and the loot made on it was all he could think about.

"I'll probably be able to drop by and talk to Coach Hicks."

"I'll check you later then."

Once the brief conversation ended, they continued to saunter towards their classes. Gossip about Silky's attire spread throughout the school. He had become extremely popular, especially with the girls. His popularity traveled to other schools as well. Some of his fans disputed over who would do his schoolwork for him.

That was petty stuff though, pelf and pegging to get it was his hang up. The streets were calling his name, and he planned to answer big time.

As soon as school was dismissed, he headed to the gym. Princess picked up her pace when she noticed him ahead of her. The cheerleader tapped him on the shoulder when she positioned herself in range.

"Remember me?" Her smile was innocent yet attractive.

"How could I forget you? You gave me the new name that I like." They slowly moved forward.

"You certainly wear it well; that suit too I might add."

"Thank you aww…"

"Princess, my name is Princess."

They shook hands, her hand wasn't released right away though. He held it and stroked it, like a lovable pet. His tender actions sent amazing chills through her body. She silently thought, "He knows what he's doing to me."

Princess snatched her hand when she began to quiver. A passionate sigh involuntarily escaped her lungs. "Ah."

The smooth player asked, "What's wrong?"

She surely didn't want him to know that he had that kind of effect on her. Pride kept her from approaching him before, today pride was kicked to the side.

The cheerleader tried to vastly regroup. She tried her best to sound believable when she spoke.

"Nothing's wrong, you just caught me off guard."

They stood still for a moment before entering the gymnasium.

"I would love to call you sometimes Princess."

The comely pony smiled from ear to ear.

"Would you really?" Her excitement was too hard to contain. Her obvious exhilaration flattered him.

"Write it down and see."

The petite nymph with the athletic build eagerly scribbled her phone number down, then shoved the torn paper towards him. After accepting the number, she was assured a call.

"I'll give you a buzz later on."

While restlessly stroking her hair she replied, "Okay."

Princess then entered the gym. Her newest acquaintance hesitated momentarily to be discreet, holding his head high as usual upon entry. Basketball was gradually becoming secondary to him. The cheerleader captain added to the brightness of his day.

Consulting with the coach and burning rubber was his present mission. The veteran coach could tell that his star player wasn't practicing this day either.

"How are you coach?"

"I'm alright. The question is how are you?"

Coach Hicks' curiosity and disappointment was obvious.

"I have some business to take care of today coach."

"Okay, just remember that's two days in a row. We need to keep winning now."

He sounded skeptical of his player's actions.

"We will Coach Hicks, you'll see."

Silky Black turned to walk off.

"Hey Leon."

"Yea Coach."

"Nice threads."

"Thanks Coach."

  The born hooper strutted on out of the gym. Princess watched through the corner of her eyes. She really had something to cheer for now, after almost melting when he caressed her hand. The team and the coaches were strongly hoping that Leon "Silky Black" Townsend wasn't thinking about quitting. Was he?

  The desire for progress led him to the office, with intentions on using the phone. A hateful secretary was seated near the door.

"May I help you?" A noticeable grunt proceeded.

"May I use your phone please?"

  The difficult woman looked up at him for the first time. Previously, her head was down while reading. An unpleasant remark was about to naturally flow; however, his professional appearance led to her continence.

"Go ahead, but no long-distance calls please."

"Thank you miss."

The word please seldom leaves her lips, especially when dealing with students. He moved with speed, attempting to act before she changed her clickable mind. The car phone rang in Mr. Wonderful's car.

"Talk to me."

"How are you mister?"

The student tried to talk without annoying the staff members.

"I'm okay youngblood. What's happening?"

"Are you busy?"

"Nawgh, just cruising, hoping to find a new catch that's all." Mr. Wonderful didn't do drugs, but his cool always seemed to make him sound high."

"Can you pick me up from school?"

"No problem, I'll be in the front."

"I'll be waiting."

The receiver was placed back on its base.

"Thank you, mam."

The secretary remained silent. The youngster flirted with a few girls down the hall. Phone numbers filled his pockets with ease. Soon the importance of them calling him became evident. Learning about females was part of his new job, therefore interaction with them was inevitable.

While standing and waiting on his ride, the absence of his own vehicle began ailing him more and more. An eye-catching automobile came into view. "That's a marvelous way to show up." The thinker had no time for quandary.

He knew what he wanted and knew he could get it. The showy car pulled up to retrieve its passenger. The onlookers were bedazzled by such a sight. The apprentice hopped in with a strong quest for knowledge, the kind that could only come from someone like the driver.

Students were still scattered out and hanging around.

"All of these hot lil numbers running loose, man I know you'll be rich soon."

The driver began to press the gas pedal.

"So how was yo' day lil bro?"

"It was cool, uplifting you know?"

"Don't I? I remember when I first got in the game, how good it felt. It's a *wonderful* feeling."
He obviously flattered himself.

"I totally agree because this suit did some wonders for me today. I had one of the main cheerleaders going nuts today."

"You gotta break her too man. The better yo' girls look, the more dough you get. Make her feel special but let her know that you don't need her. Dig?"

"I can dig it."

"Let her sample yo' flavor, then make her beg for it."

"The idea alone gives me a rush."

"It should young brother."

They were creeping along while talking.

"I want you to teach me about the track."

"Sounds like you're on the right track Jack. I was planning on showing you some stuff anyway."

"You're the driver."

They began to simper, enjoying their new friendship. The extravagant leopard seats and deep shag carpet were signs of a major player.

"I'm gonna drop the top so when the girls on the track see us, they'll know that a new mack is on the scene."

Silky liked that idea. The convertible top gradually came down and folded up behind them as they slowly rolled. The tawny upholstery was fully exposed now, along with the occupants.
The windows were fully lowered next.

## Chapter 5: School is In

The fascinated viewers made them feel like they were in an amazing parade. The driver was used to this; his buddy was experiencing a brand-new feeling. It elated him so, giving him extra incentive to push forward with his plans. The expensive, new, customized car turned on Jensen Drive.

The passel of streetwalkers wouldn't appear until later, still a few were working now.

"Pay close attention now. Most of the girls won't be out until dusk or shortly after. As you can see, a few are already clocking."

Mr. Wonderful saw a hooker that he had been trying to hook, so he tooted the horn. "Bump bump." The sassy quean tried to ignore him.

"I'll get her one day."

Leon was trying to learn so questions arose.

"What's so special about her?"

"That skinny Minnie is a nonstop mule if I ever saw one. When you get a few workhorses like that, you'll be on top for real."

The driver vainly patted his small afro that was dyed dark brown.

"That heifer lives on the track, anytime I show up she's working."

A sharp hunger pain made him voice his next thought.

"Let's go eat somewhere. Are you hungry?"

The blunt pain made him grip his stomach.

"I could always use some good food."

"We'll come back to the stroll when it's happening."

Nene's Soul Satisfaction Restaurant was their next stop. It was a small family business like most soul food cafes. The owner and cooks were originally from Louisiana, bringing some spice to Texas. The crowded hut was located on Cavalcade.

The elegantly dressed duo made their entrance. The aroma made their hunger worse. They went directly to the cashier.

"May I help you?"

The well-preserved senior citizen presented a homely smile.

"How are you mam?"

"I'm fine baby."

She bashfully waved him off, indicating flattery by him asking. Mr. Wonderful proceeded with his order.

"I'll have some spicy turkey necks, black-eyed peas with okra, mustard greens, and dirty rice."

All the orders came with cornbread. Silky Black stepped up when his comrade moved to the side.

"I'll take some Cornish hen, sweet corn, mashed potatoes, and green beans."

"Would you two like something to drink?"

"I'll take some homemade lemonade."

"Me too."

"What about dessert guys?"

They both looked at each other, then simultaneously said, "Peach cobbler." Everyone that heard them was tickled; it even tickled them a bit. The elder of the two offered to pay for both meals by handing the cashier a large bill, but Silky dug in his pocket and paid for his own.

They sat in an area designated as the official smacking zone. Pictures and posters of famous musicians and other celebrities that had previously dined there lined the walls. Shortly after being seated, the players were smacking along with everybody else.

Customers always received helpful servings of the delicious food. Thus, repetitive visitors were the well-anticipated result. The players discussed the game while chomping.

"The game ain't for everybody Silky Black, but I know you can be one of the greatest. It gives me great pleasure to be a part of yo' future legacy. You'll learn the track in no time, macking comes naturally."

His food was pushed down with lemonade.

"I look forward to rising like the sun. I wasn't born to live an average life, no not me. Once I learn the track, I'll show you a stack."

"That's what I'm talking about youngblood."

The plates were as empty as they would get.

"Are you ready?"

"Yea, let's split."

Alligator and ostrich shoes headed towards the door. King Paul stepped through the door, rubbing his paunch, meeting the two heads on. "What it is y'all?"

"We're full as ticks."

The stout bon vivant couldn't wait to order.

"Let me kill this cow, I'll check y'all out later."

"Later."

King Paul's new, black caddy was parked next to the white one. The white one began to move again.

"We'll stop at Leroy's for a few shakes, then scope out the scene."

Silky wanted to see Mrs. Renee again anyway. Something about her drew men like a magnet. It was something about the game that kept her in the mix also. She was still able to break a trick just like in her younger days but chose to put that part of the life behind her.

Mrs. Renee was well acquainted with the streets, having the type of passion and dedication that all street kings admired. Her deceased husband, Leroy, was her ex-pimp and owner of the pool hall. When he died, she felt it was her duty to keep the place going.

Mr. Leroy was a well-respected ghetto legend known nationwide. Mrs. Renee was in her late forties and had been with Leroy for more than twenty years. The dedicated woman had seen and experienced much, making her knowledge very valuable to those in their society.

The white caddy pulled up jamming Isaac Hayes. The occupants exited the car then entered the pool hall. They made a round then headed to the bar.

"Oh, you brought my new friend back." She seemed delighted.

"Good evening." The youngster spoke.

"Hey pretty lady." His tutor spoke next. "I guess I'll swallow some more scotch."

"I'll take a virgin."

The woman began fixing their drinks. Prasilla could be seen scouring about, hoping to run across a willing trick. She noticed Silky but tried to look past, he naturally did the same.

Another lady of the night decided to see who Silky Black was by sitting next to him.
Mr. Wonderful walked off to give them some privacy. He liked the fact that the fish were biting. The chic turned towards Mr. Black and asked, "Are you pimpin'?"

"Are you working?" His response was quick.

"I'm trying to." She tried to sound enticing.

"Either you are working or not."

"Yea, I'm working but I need to make some ends."

"You sure do, talking to me." His comment was stiff.

    The female appeared to be quite disappointed as she removed herself from the stool. Her smile turned upside down. He gently grabbed her arm attempting to halt her; this pleased her.

"Meet me here tomorrow at this same time, with some money. By the way, I'm Silky Black."

    He slowly released her.

"My name is Dana." She quickly added. "You didn't even ask if I had a man or not."

"That's because I don't care. After tomorrow you'll be my girl anyway."

"I'll be here." She assured him.

    A pleasant smile occupied her face again as she walked off. The tutor promenaded back to the bar. He eagerly tapped his student for information.

"So, what it be like?"

"I told her to meet me here tomorrow with some bread, at this same time."

"Right on." He grabbed his chin as a thought became clear. "You know what?"

"Hit me."

"That lil chic be working on the Southside a lot. That's probably where she lives right now. After we roll through over here, we can spin out there. Come on, let's get in the wind."

The driver used his car phone to call his house. "Are y'all ready?"

"We're just waiting on you daddy."

"Ok, I'm on the way."

The flashy man guided the car to his house. He lived in a more expensive area a few miles outside of Fifth Ward.

"I gotta swing by my pad and grab these girls."

The passenger just nodded and leaned back. Shortly after, the homeowner occupied his driveway. It was a newer brick house with ornate detail, nicely trimmed hedges, and neatly manicured evergreen grass. His women must have smelled him; they gaited out immediately.

Four prancing ponies headed towards their divine dictator. The proud man said, "Let them fill up the back." The novice cleared the way for the pretty ponies. Once they were all in, the car was in motion again.

Most of the ride back was quiet. Music from the radio made up for that. Some song that kept saying, shake your booty was on. As soon as the girls stepped out of the car, they did just that. It was a nice view for admirers of well-shaped, promiscuous women in skimpy clothes.

They marched into position, aiming to add cash to big daddy's stash. Their coordinator paused at the corner for a while, giving his troops a chance to position themselves.

Then he spoke, "Let's see what we can see, shall we."

The prosperous pander steered the car around the corner. Hookers were everywhere. Silky was utterly amazed.

"Man…it must be at least fifty hoes out here!"

"You ain't seen nothing yet."

More females lined the street as they went, profiling on both sides. The driver began lacing him up.

"You see those hoes over there to the left?"

The driver slightly tilted his head, without drawing attention.

"Yea, I see."

"Those are Luscious Larry's girls. He has a nice stable."

Silky agreed with a simple hand gesture while taking mental notes. The Cadillac rolled by slow, giving the growing young man a chance to evaluate things.

"Look over there. There's a dark alley where some of the girls run to when the pigs come through.

Most of the time they let them work, but every now and then they make a bull**** sweep. If one of yo' girls get clamped, always go get her."

Eyes glanced in the panoramic rearview mirror. The talk of cops made many uneasy. However, being cautious was key to survival. He instilled that into his women, encouraging his protégé to do the same.

Silky enthusiastically verbalized, "Those must be Pink Paradise's chics."

The man beside him jokingly asked, "What gave them away?"

"The pink roses in their hair."

They both grinned at the pink passion bit yet would never disrespect his game. They respected him and his uniqueness; his taste was just considered a little bizarre. The eccentric styles and tastes are what usually attracts their women. Therefore, the odd differences add to their appeal respectively.

The lesson continued. "That's one of my ex-girls right there. I didn't trust her, so I got rid of her. Never jeopardize yo' operation like that, it's not worth it."

One night of scanning the blade was just the beginning. "Let's fly across town for a second. I'm going to show you where that broad be at." The accelerator received more pressure.

The gangster white walls rolled hardily. The chrome rims and fancy chrome accessories shined in the night lights. The bumper kit and belts highlighted the rear end, while the superfly headlights and grill beautified the front, the chrome lady led the way.

Downtown is what separates Fifth and Third Ward, so once it was crossed their destination was upon them. The customized El Dorado reached Dowling Street, to the inquirer's surprise it resembled Jensen Drive. Hookers were everywhere, fat, skinny, nicely shaped, tall, short, and various races.

Customers drove through on a nightly basis purchasing sex. It was a very lucrative business. Many who could afford it seemed to give it a try. Everyone wanted a piece of the action, even Johnny Law. Politicians, lawyers, doctors, musicians, and the masses spent money with these women.

They were hopping in and out of cars left and right. The nonstop action filled the eyes and mind of the passenger. He felt he had to take his proper place in this. Whether it be a jaunt or trek, the lad wanted to voyage down that road.

So many of the things desired seemed to one day be within grasp. Leon never felt that feeling before. Mr. Wonderful pointed out certain things that needed to be known while creeping down the action-filled street.

The Townsend residence became the next stop, the fifteen-year-old still had to attend school the next morning. Before the night ended, the young Silky Black sat on the bole near his beloved peach tree.

The short skirts, Mr. Wonderful's nice house, lavish living, and busy streets crowded his mind. The towering teen dearly wanted to find his niche, knowing that time and experience would soon reveal it all. Staying active was essential, knowing that doing nothing would bring nothing.

The next day, the load from last night was still heavy on his mind. He debated on wearing another suit, in conclusion a suit was placed on his body. Fortunately, Charlotte was available again.

Earl Jr. didn't have to work that day, but she appeared anyway. Eugene had left already, but Earline and Leon took advantage of the ride. Earline was dropped off first. When they reached Wheatley, Charlotte playfully hit Leon on the shoulder and said, "Don't give the girls too much trouble ok."

He quickly countered with a bon mot. "It ain't about what I give them, it's about what they give me."

The weak-kneed hussy smacked her lips then playfully yelled in contempt, "Close my door boy!"

The articulate youngster obliged, then she sped off. Once again, the professional attire sparked conversation all around the school. Silky Black was making his mark as the Jovan Musk cologne left a fragrant trail.

The males were eager to shake his hand, while the females were eager to hug him, to say the least. His fan base had spontaneous growth. The person of interest sported a taupe suit on this day. His body was at school, nonetheless his mind went far and beyond.

Girls that tugged at him the hardest were considered potential prospects for the track.
The planner orchestrated brief one on one interviews with each one. He wasn't worried about the ones that would derail, the thing was to get the train moving. Sudden action was of greater importance than longevity at this point. Things would be easier to control and maintain once a steady flow was created.

The future taskmaster was cleverly trying to put it all together. The end of the school session seemed to come fast that day. The dominant starter rushed to practice, missing two days in a row already. He was letting the streets interfere with basketball.
Without any doubt he felt the streets could catapult him into a better living situation.

It didn't occur right away that basketball could do the same. He was playing strictly for the love of the sport. Coach Hicks and the team were glad to see the star player at practice. Leon tried to clear his head while practicing. Princess eyeballed the player right along with other interested cheerleaders. The hooper executed the same rhythm as usual, his moves were a treat to basketball lovers.

The locker room was bombarded instantly after practice. Leon was one of the first to enter, making his way to the shower. He rapidly scrubbed and rinsed himself. His ride was already waiting outside. A cute seventeen-year-old was standing near the eye-catching car talking to the driver.

"There's my homeboy right there. You can give yo' number to him, it's all family."

The tired student climbed in the automobile, then the hot girl handed him her number.

"What's your name?"

"Sabrina."

"Sabrina I'll be in touch."

She was biting her lip throughout their conversation, then timidly waved when the car began to roll.

Mr. Wonderful boasted, "That's one in the bag. I want to see that little jenny put some bread in yo' pocket."

The teen appreciated the effort, but he wanted to pull his own girls. As for now, it was all about getting things started. Better clothes and mediocre jewelry showed him how much material things meant to some. He could imagine the effect of the cars, houses, and other goodies.

Sabrina would have gladly jumped in the car and performed whatever was requested without a second thought. Leon Townsend was sure of that. It was as if his thoughts were plastered on his forehead, because Mr. Wonderful advised, "Get yo' tools together lil brother, and they will eat from your hand."

The tools spoken of were material possessions that fascinated the misguided and curious. The more consumed, the more it was desired. The enthused was getting higher and higher without the use of drugs. The man with the tailor-made suit on schooled his young pupil while turning corners.

"Aren't you supposed to meet that dame at Leroy's tonight?"

"Yea, at about eight o'clock."

"I'm gonna put my girls down early tonight, cause it was a little slow last night." The tutor glanced at his timepiece. "Stella did good, the rest were alright."

Before Silky realized it, they were at Mr. Wonderful's residence. He rubbed his eyes and stretched his arms.

"I must've dozed off."

"You were out like a light."

"Practice wore you out huh?"

"I guess so. We have another game Friday."

"I'll be there, I'm sure."

The happy herd marched towards the car. The tired teen stretched again when he stepped out to let the girls in. Smells from sweet perfume accompanied the gathered group. For the glittering glamour girls, it was time to go to work.

The sounds of soul music electrified the crew on the way to get daddy's pay. Good music seemed to always make things better. The youthful rider stayed alert during the trip back. The destination was Leroy's after the girls were put down.

A well-respected, older player named Mr. Willy was there, which made it busier than normal that night. He was one of Mr. Leroy's closest friends, now using a wheelchair. Word of his presence spread fast, compelling many to stop by.

His condition prevented him from appearing more often. The street legend was in his mid-sixties still selling game. Many players stopped by to pay homage. They shoved him small stacks of money left and right. Mr. Wonderful introduced Silky Black when he approached. They shook hands.

"How are you Mr. Willy?"

"I'm wonderful, Mr. Wonderful."

They both cracked a smile. The seasoned pander proudly placed four hundred dollars in the older guy's palm. Mr. Willy quickly stashed the loot.

"Thank you, player."

"Mr. Willy this is Silky Black, he's probably the youngest mack around."

"Pleased to meet you." They shook hands.

"Likewise."

Even though he didn't know the man, he still wished his pocket held enough cash to peel a wad off for him. Which was for honoring the pioneers and the love of the game. He promised himself to be able the next time he saw him.

Mr. Willy's friend offered to buy him a drink, but he declined. Silky headed towards the bar.
He stopped midway into his stride because someone called him.

"Silky Black." The voice was deep and husky.

He slowly turned around; it was Mr. Willy. Once the youngster fully focused on him, the older man told him, "Represent the game."

The developing dude nodded in acknowledgement. His comment added to the young man's confidence. He was surprised that the old man remembered his name. A buxom broad sitting near the bar caught his eye. It was Dana looking extremely uncomfortable, so her rendezvous partner approached with caution.

"What's wrong?"

"I don't want to be here." Her facial expressions and body language were telling it all.

"How did you get here?"

"I drove my jalopy."

"Let me tell my homeboy the deal, then we can split."

Dana aimlessly stirred a nearly empty drink she sipped on while waiting. Leon's alter ego found his ride.

"I'm going to roll with this chic and see what's shaking and make sure she ain't faking."

"I can dig it. Give me a buzz and watch the fuzz."

"Later." They shook hands.

Silky clenched her hand, guiding her towards the front door. She wanted to be guided by a man, the right man. The wandering lamb was driving a twelve-year-old Buick with a few kinks in it. Once in the parking lot she announced, "It's over here."

The gifted athlete trailed her to the car. Their eyes were stuck on each other while getting in. Nothing changed once they were inside. Dana wanted to enjoy a serene environment.

"Can we go somewhere quiet?"

"I don't see why not." Their beaming eyes finally veered off.

"Let's get a room, I'll pay for it."

"Drive on."

The twenty-year-old woman pulled into a motel called the Relax Inn. Minutes later, they walked into room twenty-two. They both sat on the bed after locking the door. She had on a multi-colored body dress with matching boots. Her hair was in a bob, while triple layered earrings hung from her ears.

Light brown skin enveloped her frame, with sparse freckles in her face. She was about 5'5, 130 lbs., and well-shaped. Her relaxed thighs and well-rounded curves were very inviting, but he wasn't here for that. She took her earrings off. A small lamp provided the only light desired.

The strangers tried to get acquainted.

"Look, I know you're kinda young that doesn't bother me. Honestly, how old are you?"

"Would you believe me if I tell you?"

Dana shrugged her shoulders. "I don't know, try me."

"Fifteen."

"Hell nawgh!" She jumped out of bed while yelling. "Boy, are you crazy? You cannot be serious."

She really hoped he wasn't, but he was. She waited for him to say he was playing, yet he never did. The overwhelmed broad calmed down.

"Damn, so you serious huh?"

"I'm as serious as can be." He held his poise.

Dana took a deep breath, exhaled, then went into deep thought. Her companion chose to stay silent while she collected her thoughts. She pulled off her boots without parting her lips. Next, her dress was pulled over her head, and off her body. Her panties and bra were the only garments preventing her from being naked.

"What are you doing?" He asked.

She remained silent, attempting to seduce him. When she threw herself on him, he threw her right off. Silky Black flipped the red bone on her back, pinning her to the mattress.

"Dana I'm not here for this. If this is all you want, you can take me home. I thought you wanted a man."

"I do." She sounded sad.

"Then where's the money?" His attitude was smooth.

The defeated dame sighed hard. "Let me get it."

He released her, then the frustrated fawn grabbed one of her boots and held it upside down while shaking it. A small knot fell out. She shook her head from left to right while handing him the money. The scratch was counted right away; it was a hundred and fifty in small bills.

Dana crawled up under the sheets into a ball. Silky retired his top clothing then crawled in beside her once the cash was stashed. He comforted her by cuddling her. The distressed damsel began to vent as she held him.

"I don't want to be mistreated anymore. I'm a good girl, I deserve better. I chose you because we can build together. I don't want any of those other pimps. I want a man that can appreciate me.

One that knows I care about him and can make a difference. I want to build, a man that has it all will never see me for me, so I choose you. We going to come up baby, just watch and see!" A couple of tears rolled from her eyes.

Dana seemed sincere, howbeit time would tell. It was difficult for him to keep his hands off her. "It feels so good, you holding me and all." Their lips became contiguous. The soft, passionate embracement pleased her.

"I'm not used to this."

"Me either." He refused to share how good it felt though.

She asked, "If I do everything you want me to do, will you make me happy?" She reclaimed the initial eye contact.

"Will you do everything I want you to do?"
His eyebrows were raised.

Dana spoke, making a solemn promise. "Yes, Silky Black I will do *everything* you want me to do."

"If what you say is true, I'll make you happy."

The warm woman took a deep breath. "I don't plan on letting you down. I work very hard, and I'll work harder for you."

The broad with the bodacious body seemed to be getting at something. Her new man was tired of her beating around the bush.

"What's up Dana, what's really on your mind?"

It was time to transform her whim into reality.

"Silky Black I've been banged and banged and banged again. None of it meant anything to me, it was strictly business. I want to be explored by a man that I care about, and cares about me. I chose you as my man and I need my man right now.

I don't feel this way often so don't worry. I am in need now though."

Dana immediately put her new man on the spot. He was faced with a tough decision. It was proven that sex wasn't a weakness of his, was he further being tested? Was her request and desire sincere? If so, would her duties be fulfilled as solemnly promised? He didn't want to blow a good one.

## Chapter 6: Crown Me

Silky Black made his mind up, then began removing her remaining garments. His hands became busy unsnapping her bra. Hard nipples centered the alluring melons before their release. The sensitive teats were now very visible and poking out like the tip of a pinky finger.

The longing woman aided him with the discarding of the loose bra. Her well-rounded bosoms demanded the attention received. While hoisting her shapely legs up, her burning body was freed of the damp underwear.

Her partner threw the rest of his clothes away from the bed. Two naked people occupied the bed in room twenty-two. It suddenly occurred to him that he wanted her too, while dragging his tongue along the curves outlining her anatomy.

She squirmed and squealed while her new man tended to her. The delicate tingling was a la-di-da feeling that Dana had to intensify.

Her emollient tongue flip-flopped all over his body. Before long the lean lad was being served like never before. Then, the athletic warrior grabbed his bloated spear, thrusting himself in the fluent karst! Dana gleefully received him as her spate seemed to echo around the room. They were busy most of the night.

Dana felt a feeling that she never felt before. Tears of joy rolled from her eyes, as her body seemed to lock up. The vast feeling made her have minor convulsions! Afterwards, they both laid motionless for a while. She was speechless with wide eyes, trying to figure out what had just happened.

When he touched her, she flinched hard, then scooted away from him. Her drained body was weak and wet. The flabbergasted female slammed her fist against the bed and shouted, "Damn!"

"What's wrong Dana?"

She held her silence again. Tears continued to fall as she curled up into a ball. The thinker contemplated his next move while stretched out on the side of her.

Ten or fifteen long minutes passed by without change. Dana fleetly turned around and embraced her lover without saying a word. Shortly after, the tired pair fell asleep. When dawn came birds could be heard chirping outside. Leon Townsend suddenly awoke. For a moment or two he forgot where he was.

His overexerted body had shut down without approval. Thoughts raced through his head against the clock. "I fell asleep, I've been here all night. School….I need to go to school." He shook Dana, who was so comfortable with her arm wrapped around him. He shook her a little harder to no avail.

She subconsciously sighed with closed eyes and a wide smile. An audible effort became necessary. "Dana wake up. Dana! Wake up!" Last night's episode seemed to have continued in her dream. The rash awakening caused her to simultaneously open her eyes, gasp, and cringe.

One of her hands quickly covered the left side of her chest as if to stop her heart from jumping out. "Whew, boy you scared me!" Her eyes were still buck.

There was no time for small talk. "Clean yourself up so we can go. I need to go to school." Dana reacted instantly like a good girl was supposed to. The twenty-year-old quickly showered with intention of not upsetting him. When she exited the shower, he entered it.

The freckle face fowl had a newfound energy source powering her now, it was Leon "Silky Black" Townsend indeed. While drying off the surprising stud stated, "Practice already had me tired, then you finished me off." The statement came with an intentional smirk.

The acute gesture caused her to bashfully giggle. Without stammering she starkly responded. "Last night was my first time needing you, and I must say that you took very good care of me."
While speaking the jaunty woman approached him.

The pretty pony now stood directly in front of him. With keen eye contact she spoke. "Now I'm going to take very good care of you." The proud person leaned towards him, issuing a smack on the cheek. He accepted it along with her oath.

She would work hard, for a dearth wouldn't do. They headed out the door once fully dressed.

A Scandinavian employee waved at them as they departed. Once reaching his home, Dana waited for him to change clothes. Her passenger dashed back outside with some of Ruthy's combination creations on.

He was running a tad bit late. The driver was still shocked at her new man's age. Nonetheless, she happily began to go with the program. Her young hunk was very appealing to her. The Buick pulled up at the neighborhood high school.

"Can you pick me up later?"

"Sure, what time?"

"About four thirty."

"I'll be here."

"Don't forget."

"I won't."

"Cool."

The tardy student opened the door, jumped out, then closed it. His feet then trod the pavement leading to the school entrance, as the Buick slowly pulled off. It was time to go collect some bread for her man. A frolicsome custodian spoke while performing his daily duties.

"Good morning Silky Black."

"Good morning, Lucky."

The new moniker had spread fast, the fire behind it was rapidly growing. Progress with his new lifestyle and trade seemed inevitable. Tralydia had a question that soon became popular among the girls.

She inquisitively asked him, "How can I get a glitter girl t-shirt?"

She licked her lips as to inveigle. He predicted this, as a matter of fact it was cleverly planned. Traps were set and bait was cast. The surrounding fish were biting hard too. The orchestrator slyly responded to her question.

"You have to become a glitter girl."

"What does that consist of?"

"It consists of you doing some things for me."

"Like what?"

"Like putting some bread in my pocket."

"And how do I do that?"

A devilish grin surfaced on his face. "That depends on what you want to do."

Tralydia started having second thoughts then quickly ended the curious questionnaire. "I...I don't know right now." The jittery girl nervously walked off. The player just shook his head and moved on.

When he ran into Shirley and Margie, they were given simple instructions. They attentively listened swearing to comply. Silky snuck a kiss in on Princess's jaw when he crept up on her.
The passionate play excited the limber lily.

The light-skinned doll turned red with uncontrollable blushing. The girls standing beside her marveled at the sight. The teenage sex symbol moved on without saying a word. Princess wanted to talk to him but understood that he was a busy person. Being in demand was all a part of the plan.

As long as he was in demand, those that demanded him would supply him. Extra curious girls like Tralydia were expected to eventually capitulate. Mr. Wonderful told him, "Curiosity kills the cat and makes the Mack fat." His fast-learning pupil took that piece of game and ran with it.

The hip hooper didn't want to go to practice but went anyway. Their next game was the following day, and the rising star didn't want to get cocky. Practice went well as usual. Coach Hicks encouraged the team to keep winning, he wanted to see that happen more than they could imagine.

When the Townsend kid viewed his normal pickup area Dana was patiently waiting. He swiftly skated her way, his cool walk added to his appeal. Before he was even situated in the seat, a couple of small bills were placed in his hand. The new chic was a plus.

The lad was beginning to keep a little money now. Dana was instructed to pass by the track before dropping him off. The youngster looked and learned without admitting to his lack of knowledge. During their short ride she did most of the talking, exactly what he wanted her to do.

They showed up at Leon's house at dusk.
"I'll be back tonight." She was given a thumbs up. When he walked into the house the car drove off. A special visit was made to Ruthy's room.

"Big Sis I have something for you."

"Oh yea, what's that?"

A small amount of cash was handed to her. It was accepted with a big smile.

"Thank you."

"No, thank you Ruthy."

She was glad to see her baby brother making moves.

"Hopefully, much more will come soon. I need some more glitter girl shirts too."

"That's no problem."

Earline sat quietly with open ears and eyes.
Their brother talked a bit more before leaving the room. Later that night, Dana returned as promised. She boldly knocked on the door. Earl Jr. answered it with a grumpy attitude.

"Who is it?"

"It's Dana here for Leon."

When the door opened, he was spellbound, mentally undressing her without realizing it. His gawky amazement caused her to become impatient. "Is he here?" Earl Jr. moved to the side without saying a word. Subsequently, the visitor entered the house and sat in the nearest seat. The gawky doorman retrieved Leon from their room.

"You have company Leon."

"Thanks."

The guest was greeted and escorted outside.

"Let's step outside."

The other siblings peeked out of the window at their brother's new girl. "Let me see." "Wait!"

They sat in the car and talked for a while.
"I didn't get a chance to pull nothing yet baby, but I'll have something for you tomorrow."

"Are you coming to my game tomorrow?"

"Am I your woman?"

He embraced her then kissed her on the neck. She responded by swiftly planting her lips on his. "Pick me up from school at two-forty-five."

"Anything you say baby."

    Rugged influence wasn't necessary at this point. The youth returned to his room upon entering. Dana returned to the melee of the blade.
Upon graduation a guy by the name of Gorgeous George changed her life. He appeared to have multiple personalities. She would be handed a bouquet of roses, before even being able to appreciate them he might smash them in her face.

    He literally drug her across the country, abusing her from city to city. The violent man was considered a gorilla pimp, lacking the charm and intellect that some had. The sexy streetwalker had horrible memories of this man.

    He wasn't from Houston but frequented it. The turmoil experienced with the demented man emphatically jarred her. It had only been a year since her neck was free of his grip. Earline, Eugene, and Leon walked to school together the next morning. Earline continued alone at their parting point.

It was now Friday, the next big game day. There was a highly anticipated pep rally after school. The hyperactive crowd packed the gym, cheering the band and cheerleaders on. Everyone yearned for another victory. The pep rally served its purpose well; the team spirit and fan support were tremendously high.

Many that weren't previously involved were all in now, teachers and other staff came alive. It was no secret; Silky Black was the undeniable core giving the team their beautiful edge. The noisy crowd poured out of the gym when the festivities ended. Happy feelings filled the air as the band paraded through the animated spectators, which was the grand finale.

Shirley and Margie stayed close to their man as they were told. Silky casually interacted with the fans while advancing towards the parking lot. After the familiar car was spotted, the planner headed in that direction along with his girls. They all piled in with obvious excitement.

"This is Dana y'all. Dana this is Shirley and Margie."

"Hello sisters."

"Nice to meet you, Dana."

They all shook hands. Seconds later, they were on the move. The young mack spoke to his followers.

"Dig this y'all, we all family here. Each one of you is my woman. We are all combined for the purpose of living a better life. Can y'all dig it?"

He looked around the car. The trio nodded in agreement.

Dana calmly added, "You know I'm down baby."

Shirley blurted, "Me too."

Margie interacted, "I'm not here for nothing."

The front seat passenger rehashed his ploy. "After the game we gonna start the train. It's time to put the train on the track, said the young mack." A vague snicker followed, being slightly tickled by his fly lingo. The newest member was an important addition to his operation. The purpose driven crew had no problem with concurring.

"Give them a quick run-down of the track Dana."

She took pleasure in doing that. The high school students listened and learned. They stopped at the Townsend residence for a while. A glitter girl shirt was retrieved for Dana. Silky called his mentor while in the house, but no one answered.

The basketball player knew not to eat anything heavy before a game, so McDonalds was suggested. The small group dined in, then moved on. The car was now in route to the upcoming game. Eventually, the sport's popularity would add to his street fame. The shrewd jock had already learned how to use fame to his advantage. With time, other means of leverage would be acquired also.

The location of the sports event had been reached, and the parking lot was getting full. The increase in the Wildcat following became noticeable to all; their purple school color was everywhere. Dana put her glitter girl T-shirt on before leaving the car. The trio boasted Silky Black's name on their chests, glittering for all to see.

Margie and Dana accompanied him on each arm, while Shirley attached herself by hooking a finger through a belt loop in the back of his pants.

Their heads were held high as they strutted about. The Jesse H. Jones Falcons were the present opponents. Both teams were undefeated thus far.

With a quick change of clothes Silky Black was in uniform and ready for the tip off. He hugged his girls before joining the team. Shortly after the contest started, Mr. Wonderful walked through the door with Pink Paradise, Too Cool Ken, and a handful of beautiful ladies.

The presence of the older macks made the youngster proud; they came to support one of their own. The fans roared when their team made notable plays. The dominant Wildcats were able to gain another win, bringing their record to 5-0. Princess led the now famous Silky Black cheers as usual. Leon's impetus was remarkable. He made sure to let his fans know they were appreciated.

Then he walked towards the older macks with gratitude, as his trio stood nearby. The males respectfully shook hands.

"That was a sensational game you played youngblood."

"Thank you."

Mr. Wonderful lowered his voice. "I like how you represent the game too. I see thirty toes in check."

"The oldest one is the dame from Leroy's."

"Right. Right." He shook his head in remembrance. "She's nice lil brother."

Too Cool Ken and Pink Paradise stepped up to congratulate the athlete.

"Good game Silky Black."

"Yea, you something else!"

They both gave him five with energetic interest.
They noticed his small stable, with their way of life it was given. Too Cool Ken threw a suggestion in the air.

"How about downing some drinks?"

"I need to put these cars on the track.
Tomorrow should be better for me." Silky responded.

"We certainly understand that." Pink Paradise cosigned.

"Yea, Silky Black get paid man."

Many eyes crossed the well-dressed group as pellucid diamonds decorated the bunch, sparkling throughout the arena. The gathered onlookers and luminaries began to disband. The hombre wearing the number five jersey walked away with his mentor.

The mentor quietly explained a few more ramifications before departing. His pupil couldn't wait to put this innovation into action. A sneak peek at the older macks gave Silky's girls a future glimpse of their soon-to-be established man; even though they weren't supposed to be looking.

It served as a form of encouragement, whereas a disloyal follower would easily be tempted to jump ship. Dysfunctional dopes and dilatory dipsticks would not do. The thinker signaled for his trio to come forth. Shirley grappled his shorts while her stable sisters each embraced an arm.

He dried off before leaving the sideline of the court, still his clothes were damp. After he briefly kicked a little politics with the locals the crew headed to the Townsend residence. The conductor briefed his team on the way and would continue to do so while in route to the track.

Everyone waited in the car while Silky washed up. Mr. Townsend was seated in the front room watching Beretta, Kojak, or some cop show, while chugging down a can of Schlitz malt liquor beer. Earl Sr. squeezed the empty can then asked, "How did it go son?"

"We won again." Leon kept walking without pause. He didn't see the conversation going any further anyway.

"How many does that make?"

"Five."

Earl Sr. grabbed another beer from the fridge, popped the top, then reclaimed his seat. Curious little Earline managed to find her way to Dana's car. She talked to the girls while Leon was in the bathtub scrubbing himself. The familiar stray cat rubbed against her legs as she babbled on.

When the prince returned, he yelled, "Girl take yo' a** in the house!"

Earline rolled her eyes and poked her lips out, then said farewell. "Bye y'all."

"Meow, meow" the cat drew his attention.

"It's time to get fat now cat." He mumbled to the feline.

The whiskered animal stood there watching the car sail off. Something caught Earline's attention that prevented her from going in right away. Charlotte and Earl Jr. pulled up arguing as usual.
Meanwhile, thoughts of handling serious business filled Silky's mind.

If his team was on point, they should be thinking the same. He issued his final pep talk for the night before giving specific instructions. Since two of the girls were fresh, he planned to stick close. It was part of his duty to oversee their actions, especially at this point. The aspiring pander tried to add to their confidence while ensuring their safety.

Many of the dictators took extreme measures to get money from the females. He was determined to earn his keep without going ballistic.
Nonetheless, piffle and grime were all a part of it. The vehicle passed through the desired area at a gradual pace, allowing the occupants to scan the scene.

The organizer gave step-by-step instructions. Once their responses satisfied him, they were sent to work. The car was then parked at the given location. The street was overflowing with perky prostitutes and automobiles clogging the way. Horns blew, doors opened and closed, heads bobbed, and currency was being transferred.

The teenager discreetly climbed a tree like a simian; it served as his hiding spot. He was able to see everything he wanted to see. After about ten minutes, someone picked Margie up. Dana grabbed a couple of tricks before the night ended. Shirley was getting discouraged but finally knabbed one towards the end of the night. When the organizer felt it was time the troops were called in.

The car was reloaded and moving again. Sitting in the tree for so long caused his tailbone to hurt. He ignored the pain by focusing on the gain. The intake was sufficient especially for the first night. The trainees were dropped off at home with another day's work awaiting. The remaining two agreed to see each other the next day. Thus, Dana dipped on home.

Being exhausted, the athlete fell asleep soon as he hit the sack. Earline was up watching Fat Albert the next morning on their black and white, two-knob television. Ruthy was the designated cook when Wilma Townsend was at work. She had the frying pans sizzling with bacon and eggs. Orange juice and toast would complete the breakfast.

Before the breakfast call Eugene decided to join Earline, Earl Jr. was somewhere sniffing Charlotte's derriere. Earl Sr. was in the front yard changing the oil in his truck, and Leon was still sleeping hard.

## Chapter 7: The Engine

It was Saturday, so many school kids could be heard hollering up and down the block.
Charlotte brought Earl Jr. back before Leon woke up, her present plans didn't include him. The sneaky pauper rushed to meet a guy named Fred, her new pill connection. Their fair exchange was already established. She walked through his door with a strange look on her face, as the host led her to the bedroom.

They began undressing right away. Freaky Fred was naked immediately; Charlotte still stood in her underwear.

"Un uh wait! Where my sh**?"

Fred pulled a tiny bag out of his drawer, then handed it to her. "Here."

It was full of pink hearts and black mollies.
A crooked smile surfaced once she accepted the pills.

"Yea fool don't play with me!"

She talked trash to feel special, a mere junkie prostitute.

The remaining pieces of clothing were peeled off. The pill popper was pleased with the contents of her bag.

"I usually don't do this, but since you hooked me up, I'm gonna hook you up. Lay down." She gently pushed him.

She lowered her head to briefly engage. Suddenly, his erotic pleasure halted.

"Un uh I can't do this…. I have a man! We can still grind though."

They wasted no time positioning themselves; soon their cheap thrill was concluded. The naked female took advantage of his cleansing facilities. Afterwards, she rubbed Fred's shag then announced,

"Come lock your door."

"When are you coming back?" He almost started panting.

"We'll see." She strode towards the front door.

Her connection instinctively followed.

"Later Fred. Maybe I'll let you have your way next time."

She blew him a kiss while heading towards her mother's car. Two pills were shoved down her throat before leaving his driveway. The appealing junkie sold pills to friends here and there, making her feel that it was well worth it.

Earl Jr. held his girlfriend in high regard; no way would he believe her promiscuous activities. She actually even gave him some change every now and then, thanks to her new hustle. The youngest brother finally woke up, then entered their stench filled bathroom. He decided to let it air out before reentering.

"A few chics called for you earlier homeboy." Eugene was high already.

"Did they leave a name?"

"I'm not yo' secretary fool!"

"Find me one then." The youngest countered.

"Whatever homeboy."

Their communication was normal for two brothers, a little trash talk here and there, nothing major. Before Charlotte came along their oldest brother carried on in the same manner. Nowadays he seems to take everything so personally.
Eugene resented her but kept it cordial for his brother's sake. She sensed it but could care less.

After brushing his chops and washing his face, the thinker went to the backyard to meditate.
The fifteen-year-old now had his feet wet; having three females on the blade at his age was impressive to his kind. Now that the team was on track, his aim was to keep them on it.

After privately brainstorming it was time to soak in the tub. While bathing hunger settled in; Nene's Soul Satisfaction sounded good. He could almost taste some of the entrees. The coach thought about his team, wondering if they were hungry. Consuming the cold breakfast was still an option hopefully.

Upon entering the kitchen, he found that to be untrue. "Who ate my food?" No one answered.

The telephone was seized next, and Dana's number was dialed, but no one picked up. Silky Black meandered through the house into the front yard in bitter frustration, with both hands raised, like a referee indicating a field goal.

Darling Dana must have sensed his frustration because she arrived promptly. Instantly, taking control of her car became mandatory. His posterior end rested on the curve bordering the yard. He stood up when she approached him.

"Hey baby." Her voice was awakening.

"What it is?"

"It's me and you all the way through." She was hip too.

"Is that right?"

"As long as you stay true, I'm gonna do what I have to do."

"I'm tired of walking Dana."

"You can use my car until we get you another one."

That was close enough to what he wanted to hear. His stomach rumbled.

"Are you hungry?"

She politely answered. "A little."

"Let's split. Nene's here we come."

He was handed the keys; the Buick had a new driver now. The owner took diligent care of the 1961 automobile, minus the small kinks. Soon the kinks would be a thing of the past. Somehow Dana received a rush from her man driving her around, it was supposed to be. The person handling the steering wheel totally agreed.

Formative ideas continued to spawn that he planned to execute with precision. Future intentions were elucidated while riding as his latest asset eagerly listened.

"Dana if we are to have things, it's mandatory to keep the girls on the track. I'm confident you'll do your part but keeping the girls in check is a part of your job too. I'm the authoritative figure here, so try to encourage them with a friendly tone."

His last statement was rehashed.

"Basically, don't try to boss the girls around. You understand?"

"I'm with you."

The suave player had an auspicious approach that would win many over. They cautiously maneuvered around a minor traffic accident in route to the modest bistro. The freshly acquainted couple swaggered into the place upon arrival. His taste buds were craving oxtails with mashed potatoes.

The other guest chose meatloaf, macaroni, sweet peas, and cranberry tea. They chewed and chewed until their bellies were full. The two were confronted by a slick talking conman with a jewelry box in his hand.

When they stepped out of the food joint he swiftly approached. "Got that jewelry baby! Men's and ladies' rings." The box was flipped open with nimble hands. "I gotta sell some quick before I have a fit. I'll give you a deal you won't believe. Just try one on."

"We'll pass." Silky was hip to the slum game.

The twosome jumped in the car then left. The driver was itching to give his mother some green, hoping tonight's take would be sufficient. The high school basketball star took a trip to the park. The visit bought some time. The fellows were glad to see their buddy and greeted him well.

He decided to play one game for old times' sake. Afterwards, he sought a telephone booth to call Shirley and Margie. Shirley was called first; both were told to be ready. The girls were promptly picked up to repeat their actions from the previous night.
Eager eyes watched from high up in a tree.

The nonstop action was unbelievable. Salacious harlots were present for the picking. High heels, dollar bills, and cheap thrills was a player's description of it all. For blocks and blocks ladies of the night lined the sides of this notorious street. Patrol cars passed through, but they ignored the obvious. Most did not bother arresting them, it was almost degrading in a way, busting a mere prostitute.

The cops equated that with arresting a kid for pelting rocks at an abandoned building.
They usually only bothered the working girls when pressure was applied from their superiors, that's when the massive sweeps came about. Margie and Shirley did what was required of them, although their nerves were still quite shaky.

After a long night the girls were called in. The fresh fish were gradually trying to acclimate; the older perch was already used to it. The chicklings didn't want to disconcert their leader, prudence was exercised by discreetly complaining to Dana.

Margie told her, "One dude was so fat, until I started not to do it."

Shirley voiced her previous hang-up, "I had one with a sour smell."

Their stable sister comforted them, snickering a little while shaking her head. "Y'all will get used to it, trust me. I've been doing this for three years already. I've been to quite a few cities around the country too."

She was eye-bawled strangely for a second.

"Really?" Margie suddenly wanted the same.

The younger two abruptly attained a sense of admiration for Dana. So far so good, things have been mellifluous. After Silky black dropped the chicklings off, he paid for a motel room. The conversation was very brief before entering dreamland. Dana took a long bath before climbing in bed.

    Once the night's take was counted it seemed suitable. They discussed some issues then fell asleep. The next day, Leon couldn't wait to give his mother some money. Wilma Townsend wasn't at home when he arrived. The pickup truck was in the driveway, but Earl Sr. was gone too.

    Ruthy was fixing Earline's hair, Earl Jr. was lying across the bed reading a comic book, and Eugene was talking to some girl on the phone. Leon asked Eugene to ride with him.

"Come ride with me."

"Where to?"

"I need to drop Dana off."

"Why not?"

Eugene hung the phone up then headed outdoors. Dana was sitting patiently in the car. Leon jumped behind the wheel again, then proceeded to drive towards Dana's house for the first time. She lived with her widowed mother, whose husband was recently killed in the Vietnam war.

The heartbroken woman's sorrow was obvious, whereas Dana grieved in her own inconspicuous way. Her actions were assumed to be a form of rebuttal regarding her father's death. The broad automobile pulled up at the small Sunnyside home.

"I'll pick you up about seven."

"Ok." She unlocked the front door and went in.

Her young hunk released the brakes and continued. Eugene slapped his leg while shouting, "Man you got her! That one is a super fox; she should serve you well."

"So far so good."

"Well, I'm definitely pulling for you lil brother."

They gave each other five with pride. This teen had pecuniary concerns; fun was secondary.
Before leaving the Southside, he scanned the strip in Third Ward that Mr. Wonderful showed him.
There were a few stragglers trying to bring in some daytime funds.

Eugene was still trying to grasp the concept of his baby brother macking. He thought to himself, "I must have been getting high too long?"

Leon didn't bother to explain his actions, knowing he wouldn't fully comprehend anyway.
Peach air freshener was sprayed as they entered the freeway in route to Fifth Ward. Riding and strategizing suddenly became easier as the pleasing scent refreshed him.

Eugene was dropped off at a freak's house, then Leon coasted home. The main face he wanted to see was there this time.

"Hey Mama."

"Hey Leon."

Wilma's son pulled a stack of cash out of his pocket and gave it to her.

"Here Mama take this."

"Boy where did you get this?"

"I've been helping some people out, doing odd jobs."

"Make sure you fly right son." A peculiar look claimed her face.

It gave him joy when she accepted the bills. Next, his current focus was shifted to Ruthy. He encouraged her to make exotic clothing for men and women that his revenue would contribute to. He aimed to generate the support of street players and everyday consumers with a specific taste.

He noticed Ruthy teaching Earline things about her trade. He knew that leading by example was the key. It was 6:30 already and Margie's phone was staying busy; Shirley couldn't come outside. Her parents felt she stayed out too late the previous nights. The caller was disappointed yet moved on.

He pulled up at Dana's house around seven as planned. When she hopped in, he updated her.

"That's ok I'm used to working by myself anyway."

They headed to Margie's in hopes of retrieving her.

"Go get her."

Dana softly knocked on the door, then Margie speedily exited. Once inside the car, they drove to acquire bare necessities for the tasks at hand. Dana knew the average guy wouldn't accept her job requirements, thus someone like Silky was desired.

Sunday night was just like any other on the whore-infested street. Margie and Dana strutted down the avenue, wagging with the rest. Their instructor cloaked a different way this time, tired of monkeying around with trees.

A Spanish guy pulled up on the side of them. After Dana responded to his offer, she was signaled to get in with a hand gesture. Both girls took turns riding off. Silky pulled Margie out early, considering she had school the next day. He didn't want her to be grounded too.

Ten toes were kept down while Margie was being dropped off. She handed over the night's take without pother.

"I hope you keep being a good girl cupcake."

The remark caused her to timidly blush while playfully covering the exposed side of her face. With one stroke his hand passionately caressed her neck and breasts. Margie's head fell into the center of his chest. The cunning individual held his lamb for a moment or two, kissed her on the forehead, then sent her in.

"Go get some rest."

She hesitated before lifting her head.

"We'll see each other tomorrow."

"Hmm…" She took a deep breath, the desire to stay was painted well.

The passenger door was unlatched, opened, exited, then closed again as tired feet moved away. Once the lamb was safely inside tires screeched away. Comforting the crew was essential, failure to do so would surely lead to a total fiasco.

Leon scooped Dana up and headed home.

"Pick me up after school."

"That's not a problem."

Now everyone had parted ways for the night. Before falling asleep Shirley's absence was dwelled on for a minute. A plan had to be conjured up to keep things flowing. Dana juggled with minor issues of her own. She wanted to adorn the crew and groom her man without overstepping her boundaries.

Margie was highly intrigued by it all, her head was spinning a hundred miles a minute. She wanted to make more money, see other cities and sights. Listening to Dana prompted this and more. Margie admired Shirley's courage but personally didn't feel she belonged. Wisely, that was kept to herself.

# CHAPTER 8: MOTIVATION

Overall, Silky considered his weekend to be successful. It was now Monday, and he couldn't wait to tell Mr. Wonderful about his fair start. He phoned him before leaving with Dana. The flashy man answered.

"Hello."

"This is Silky Black, are you busy?"

"I'm just kicked backed relaxing."

He was at home leaning back in his leather recliner while getting a pedicure and massage.

"So, what's happening?"

"This weekend was cool. I had thirty toes down Friday and Saturday, then twenty down Sunday. I have to cook up a plan for one of the girls' parents. Things will go smoother when I do."

"Just make sure you stay on it, because the day you lay off, is the day it doesn't pay off. Keep some broads down no matter what.

One day you might have to work yo' neighbor, or yo' brother's ex-girlfriend. You just never know, but you must stay paid no matter what."

"I appreciate your guidance; everything will pan out just as I promised."

He couldn't wait to give him a stack.

"Your success is reward enough for me, don't ever forget that."

"I'll keep you updated; we'll rap later."

"Alright youngblood."

Once outside, Leon sat next to his oldest girl while wrecking his brain, trying to figure out how to keep Shirley working without alarming her parents. He unexpectedly began to receive massaging hands of his own across his shoulders.

"Don't have an aneurism trying to think too hard. You'll come up with something baby."

Her relaxing hands began to make a difference as his neck began receiving attention.
She discontinued only after being positive he was satisfied.

They went to pick Margie up at her friend's house, she had convinced the girl to come. The group of four headed to the work spot. The new girl was briefed and sent with the others. The poor girl was shaking like a leaf, trying her best to avoid the tricks. Silky Black felt that she would be a loose string, so he dropped the flopper back home.

Many in his position would have tried to keep her out there, but his gut told him to remove the weak link immediately. The remainder of the night met his expectations. The next day, he stumbled upon an unwanted surprise. He noticed a crowd gathered at the end of the hall at school.

Something drew him that way. While casually approaching the crowd, he noticed everyone circling around someone laying on the floor. He broke through the crowd after realizing who it was!

"Shirley! That's my girl!"

A fellow student was holding and patting her hand, attempting to revive her. The shocked player dropped to his knees while constantly asking, "What happened?"

Then he yelled, "Somebody get the nurse!"

The nurse was already alerted and on the way. Somebody finally answered him.

"She just passed out."

The concerned teens didn't know what to do.
He gently shook her body while calling her name.

"Shirley, Shirley, wake up."

She was still unconscious when the nurse arrived. The paramedics could be heard coming from a distance. Once they placed her in the ambulance, Leon climbed in beside her. The Lockharts were notified right away and arrived at the hospital shortly after she arrived.

Shirley's location stunned her once regaining consciousness. She was gratified to see her hero by her side. Her parents came into view next.

"Are you alright honey?"

Their daughter sluggishly shook her head without saying a word. Multiple weeks of barely eating had finally caught up, plus she was dehydrated.

Game six was two days away, everybody was highly anticipating it except number five. Dana and Margie carried on as usual that night, then visited Shirley the next day.

"Girl how are you?"

"We been worried about you." Margie added.

"I'm ok I guess; I just have to start eating right."

She decided to let them in on her little secret while their man was searching for a vending machine.

"I've been trying to lose some weight for our man. Don't tell him though, please…"

The sheer determination to please him impressed them, as they looked at each other with wonder. Dana encouraged the pursuit of a healthy diet.

"Nothing was wrong with your idea; you just went about it the wrong way. Listen to the doctor and follow a real diet, ok."

"We don't want you to get sick again."

"I understand y'all."

When the boss returned the visit lasted a while longer. The next day was game day again.
Shirley's present condition made number five very edgy. The maturing teen tried to contain the weird feeling hovering over him. His performance was unwanted evidence of his hang-up.

Silky Black was called to the bench, something Coach Hicks hated to do. This was the first time since making the team, to be benched for poor performance. Coach Hicks, along with the assistant coach, tried to console him without mentioning what the obvious problem was.

The Wildcats were struggling to stay in range as the opponents increased their lead. Leon helplessly watched as his immobilized body and mind soared into outer space. Abruptly, a motion picture moment took place. The impetuous crowd began chanting his name.

"Silky Black! Sil..ky Black! Silky Black! Sil..ky Black!"

Princess and the other cheerleaders joined in on the famous cheer she created.

"Silky Black! Sil..ky Black! Silky Black! Sil..ky Black!"

The fans made it known that they wanted their star back on the court. He heard their determined cry while his mind still wandered in space. Through all the loud chanting and extra hype, he heard a familiar voice straining to call him.

"Leon, Leon."

The adolescent athlete snapped out of it; turned and stood up at the unbelievable sight. There was a woman standing and waving at him, his mother. Earl Senior stood up next to her once she caught their son's attention.

The kid wearing the number five jersey lit up like a candle while waving at his parents! This was their first appearance at one of his games. He was elated and ready to play, informing the coaches immediately. Subsequently, jogging in place and rotating his arms while waiting.

Seconds later, he reentered the court. The Wildcat crowd went crazy!

"Yeeaahh! Yeeaahh!" "Hooo Hooo Hooo!"

The hooray didn't stop either because Silky Black put on a stupendous show. The other team grew weary as he continued to slam and shoot the ball through the nets. The motivation given to the other players boosted their performance also, leading to another victory.

The Townsends finally got a chance to witness their youngest son's talent in motion. After the game he rushed to greet them. They attended a few of Eugene's games in the past, so he wasn't as excited as his baby brother. He made his way towards them once Leon settled down a bit.

"Hey Mama, hey Daddy."

"Good game son." Earl Sr. congratulated him.

"Thank you, Daddy."

"You did real good Leon."

"Thank you, Mama." He could tell they were proud.

A few more words were uttered before Eugene walked up, then he was recognized too. The proud father asked, "Do y'all have rides home?"

After both brothers confirmed their rides, the hard-working couple bid them farewell. Silky kissed his mother on the cheek and surprisingly hugged his father. They then shuffled away through the crowd.

"They snuck up on you huh?"

"I knew they would come one day."

"Are you going to the after party?"

"Me and the girls might swing by there."

The brothers parted with the crowd. Silky and the crew showed up at the festivities with eyes glued to them, fingers pointing. Spontaneously, this kid went from hand-me-downs to tailor made outfits, new income, and local stardom.

"Make sure y'all enjoy yourselves."

"We will baby."

He wanted to make sure they could never say fun wasn't allowed. He was thinking about them having blisters on their feet, and him having cramps in his hands from counting money.

In his mind that would soon come, but for now he took advantage of the party scene. The girls paraded around in hot pants and other skimpy outfits with loud colors. The guys hopped around in bell bottoms, platform shoes, and busy shirts with butterfly collars. Many of the fellows imitated James Brown and other popular artists, while the gals just shook their rumps as hard as they could.

The sounds of Rick James made the crowd go wild. Sloppy teens were stumbling all over the place. The stench of vomit, sweat, reefer, alcohol, and cigarettes polluted the air. The excitement caused the smell to go unnoticed; most were eagerly adding to it anyway.

## Chapter 9: Turning Point

Shortly after Shirley's fainting incident, Leon had a heart-to-heart talk with her. He made it personal by going to her home. While standing at the end of her parents' driveway they chatted. This distance was chosen to elude any lurking listeners from inside.

"Shirley, when I saw you on the floor unconscious like that, it did something to me. It made me realize how much I really care about you. I can't afford to let something happen to you in the streets either. I don't want you on the strip anymore. I still want you to be down with me, but not like that."

"I'll always be down with you Leon."

One of her parents began calling her name. Her visitor took it as a cue to leave.

"I'll see you later Shirley."

"Ok."

He hopped in Dana's car then drove off, with much on his mind. Soon the favored peach tree would see its frequent guest again.

For the most part things seemed to be swell.

"What is this that I'm feeling?"

He tried to gather his thoughts, shake it off, and keep moving. The Wildcats were still undefeated. The star was still able to dribble on and off the court without flopping. Their record had improved to 10-0. They were to face the Lions again, who had only lost their first game. The stakes were high, and the fans loved it.

This Wildcat pep rally would take the cake. They had a stuffed lion made of cotton laying in a casket. They had a ten-minute pretend funeral for the lion, then the loud celebration began for the anticipated victory.

The Wildcats were averaging over 110 points a game, setting state and national records. KCOH radio station was making sure that everyone knew too. They weren't the only thing booming; the Arab oil embargo quadrupled oil prices in ninety days, fueling Houston's economic boom from 1973 to 1981.

When time permitted Leon took Shirley to a drive-in movie theater on SouthPark Boulevard. He just wanted to be a normal teen for a moment. They watched Cleopatra Jones while enjoying each other's company. He had a way of making each female feel special, they appreciated it too.

Basketball and his street sport seemed to be competing with one another, both demanding attention. It soon became known that becoming a glitter girl required extra duties. Leon began to realize things had to be toned down at school; he didn't want one sport to cancel out the other.

Everyone wasn't intrigued with the athletic pied piper. Disdain grew among some as the word spread of his other activities. Even though various females would approach he learned to be selective.
The booming star tried to balance, giving each sport what was required without blemishing the other.

He even toned his attire down at school, understanding the greater purpose. Coach Hicks even commended him, "I'm glad you're refocusing Leon."

Victory after victory followed each game, it was amazing to say the least. Silky Black was winning on both ends. Some of the faces changed but the game remained the same. After forty-four games they went on to win the state championship for the fourth time in six years!

They beat the Midland Bulldogs and finished the season 44-1. Eddie, Wendall, Steven, and all the players celebrated. There were 7600 people recorded in attendance. Strangely, it snowed three times that year, something totally unheard of for Houston, Texas.

Scouts were scouting and college basketball wasn't the only basketball discussed. The big leagues were looking hard. Eugene was graduating and could use any good news possible. He had options, yet most of the focus was on his baby brother.

After basketball season the hustle and bustle of the streets crowded Leon's mind. It became harder and harder to concentrate on school related business. Shirley tried her best to make him hang in there. She still managed to play her part without going on the track.

She had something she wanted to share with him when the time was right. For now, it would be kept to herself. Time was moving on; Leon copped his first ride and was seventy toes deep. In no time, he resembled and operated like the older players. When some of the older players tried to peel him, they discovered it wasn't as simple as they thought.

He even copped the skinny Minnie from the Southside that Mr. Wonderful was after. It was unbelievable to most how young Silky Black was, and the tight game he exercised. Somehow, he even managed to graduate high school.

Silky spruced Dana's car up, making it look new again. Those that couldn't fit in the car with him rode with her. When the thought weighed heavily on him, he would sporadically give Mr. Wonderful a few bills. He gave him a couple of nice stacks when he first came up but always felt led to randomly bless him.

"You surprised a lot of people, but not me. I knew you had it in you."

Leon had his own place with plush everything. Some of his girls lived with him. Silky Black was far from the little kid shooting hoops at the park. He had ventured into manhood, refusing to look back. It was something about the south side of town that kept drawing him, even though he operated all over.

Margie stayed down long enough to fulfill her wishes to travel. Dana shared what she learned on the road, and with the info given from seasoned travelers, Silky Black was ready to roll. Shirley was tasked with overseeing the girls that were staying, when Silky and the others were on the road.

All the girls would be interchanged out at his discretion. Hitting the road was considered a privilege. Therefore, he made sure Shirley traveled also. Predators and prey were everywhere. The crew found themselves in Miami. While creeping down South Biscayne Boulevard they noticed a forty-story office building recently built downtown, the One Biscayne Tower.

They docked at a motel on the strip. Silky allowed the troops to rest the first night, while he scoped out the scene. He checked the temperature of the activities abroad, surveyed, then plotted. From the looks of things their stay would be brief. After three or four nights of hitting it hard, they were on the move again.

It was 1977, Silky Black was nineteen and having it his way. Four years had passed since he first became active. They passed through Tampa after leaving Miami. All hell broke loose at Tampa Stadium while they were there. There was a riot at the Led Zeppelin Concert where rioters damaged stadium property and clashed with police.

The ruckus didn't prevent the visitors from grabbing a few dollars before moving on. The next stop was Columbus, Georgia. Skateboarding and local wrestling events captivated the community, regretfully the city still seemed to be overshadowed by crime.

The plan was to stick and move as usual, unless some other serious circumstance arose.

One of the girls had to flee from a crazy, otherwise things were fairly normal. Three months after leaving Columbus, a serial killer arose deemed the Stocking Strangler. He targeted older, solitary women in their homes, placing the whole city on edge.

Birmingham, Alabama was next on the list. A catastrophic F-5 tornado struck there two months prior to Silky's group arrival. There was a severe tornado outbreak that included twenty-two touching down in Mississippi, Alabama, and Georgia. The one that hit Birmingham was the strongest, killing twenty-two people and injuring more than one hundred thirty.

The traveler seized the opportunity to obtain a new girl then moved on. Something about Hattiesburg was calling his name. There was rich Civil Rights history there overlooked by many, including the Freedom Trail. There's also the African American Military History Museum and so much more.

An all-African American little league baseball team made a significant run to the Little League World Series that year, leaving a powerful mark in history for the region. Something strange happened, Silky took the girls on a tour, then decided to blow the whole town.

The gold 1975 Chrysler Cordoba that was purchased brand new, was on the move again with five occupants. A minor pitstop or two were made before reaching New Orleans. Once entering the city limits everyone showed some form of excitement.

"We're here." Silky shared.

"Yeah!" The new girl, Amy, lightly aired.

"Right on!" Another one added.

Once on the scene people were roaming everywhere. As soon as the troops received instructions it was showtime. Silky noticed a crowd pouring into the Tipitina's music club which hosted regular performances by local legends. New Orleans was hosting the upcoming Super Bowl, even though their sports teams weren't doing well.

"If y'all do really well, we can enjoy the town on our last day."

"Off to the races we go." They were all ears.

They consumed as much of the Cajun cuisine as allowed. After being good bad girls, certain tourist attractions were able to be enjoyed by them.
Silky phoned Shirley from a pay phone, even though he had a car phone.

"How are things going?" He asked.

"Well as to be expected. I did have to check a hoe though, she's straight now. We're stacking it up for you, don't worry."

"I know you're on top of things."

"What's new with you?"

"I copped a lil chic named Amy."

"Oh yea, that's cool."

"We're about to leave N.O., I'll probably only make a couple of stops before heading in. I'll rap with you soon. Later."

Silky had a cassette player in his customized load, which wasn't too common yet. He was digging the new station in Houston, Love 94 FM too. Shockingly to some, Silky Black still played basketball. Numerous colleges were tugging at him. There was even talk about him going pro.

The streets had all but sucked him up. Still, there were golden opportunities awaiting if so desired. Leon tried to stay fit but was drifting further from the courts. The Eastern Basketball Association was looking at him, even some with the NBA.

After the extensive road trip everyone was compelled to regain focus on making it happen in H-town. Silky Black's stacks were thicker and his stable was larger. He met a few cross-country players while out on the road. They respected each other's "P." Checkerboard Square in SouthPark was another spot where the players played.

There were thirty pool tables inside, with plenty of sticks, balls, and holes. Plenty of gambling and trash talking took place here. The owner was a businessman that fit in with the culture. He possessed many of the things they had and were drawn to.

While in the pool hall he overheard some guys talking. They were chugging down beers, drinking liquor, and smoking cigarettes. Some of the cigarettes even looked wet.

"Man, you heard what happened to Easy Money Sonny?"

"Nawgh man, what happened?"

They were all at attention as the talebearer continued.

"Some dude found out Sonny was cashing in on his sister. So, homeboy followed him to the corner store, then hopped out with a pump and blew his head off!"

"Wow!" "Whaaattt?" The fellows couldn't believe it.

Some actually cared, others just thought about pulling his girls. Silky took a deep breath, shook his head, and moved on. He wondered if Mr. Wonderful had heard the news. As fast as bad news spreads he figured as such. The tragic event took everybody by surprise.

The next day, after the news aired, the whole city heard about Easy Money Sonny's demise. Prior to this last trip all hell broke loose in Houston, when six officers brutally beat a twenty-three-year-old Mexican American who was a Vietnam war vet. After the horrendous beating they pushed him into Buffalo Bayou where he drowned!

His body was found three days later. None of the officers were convicted of a felony; two were given probation and a fine, two were granted immunity for their testimonies. All six were found guilty of violating his civil rights.

The absence of justice sparked protests and riots! Pressure from the public and concerned officials led to the creation of HPD's Internal Affairs Division to investigate police misconduct. It would take forty-four years before The City of Houston would officially apologize for the travesty.

Several civil rights protests took place in Houston that year. Significant political and social events shaped the landscape along with the swelling oil boom. Major national conferences were all part of the gumbo.

Day after day life was unfolding. Leon invited his family to his home for dinner. Only his two main girls were allowed to participate in this gathering. His relatives were impressed with his taste and assets. He made it his business to be a helping hand to all of them. His parents had mixed reactions but were still proud of him.

Earl Jr. seemed to be a bit envious but tried his best to contain it. Periodically, he tried to crack a lame joke, revealing his shallow jealousy. Even so, he would never let anyone hurt his baby brother. After a few weeks Amy disappeared. This wasn't bothersome at all; it came with the territory.

Shirley worked what the players considered a square job. Nonetheless, she always came through when needed. They saw plenty of chics coming and going, refusing to be counted amongst them. Still, the thriving mack had staying power for most.

Suddenly, the court was calling his name again. He was invited to train with several teams. Leon was very undecided about his basketball future. Consequently, the young man ventured to a familiar spot at his parents' house.

He knew he couldn't hop from team to team, so practicing away from the crowd was decided upon. Sooner than later major decisions would have to be made. Time wasn't necessarily on his side. Out of nowhere, an F-3 tornado touched down in Northeast Houston! This was Silky's area of town.

"It's time to hit the road again."

This time he took Shirley with him, and left Dana in charge of those that were instructed to stay. Margie was still around too. Even when chickens stopped clucking, at least four or five would always remain. He became known for keeping double digits in the stable.

This time Silky's compass pointed towards the Midwest. Because of the long drives, he often allowed one of the main girls to drive too. The ship sailed down I-45 North headed who knows where. He told the crew while passing through, "We'll stop in Dallas on the way back."

"Ok Silky."

They were along for the ride, and proud to be.

Upon plunging into Oklahoma, the journeyers traveled through Choctaw Nation. Other than restroom breaks and gas they kept rolling. This was Indian land without a doubt, as they rolled through Cherokee Nation.

    It was time for a rest stop again.
While approaching the entrance Silky saw something amazing and disturbing at the same time. He saw a gorgeous Cheyenne Indian dressed in tribal clothes, being manhandled and forced into a car. Of course he didn't have any idea what tribe she was from.

    Without thinking he sprung into action!
Leon Townsend blitzed the two guys, grabbing them and slanging them around like ragdolls! Then his fists began to pound them before they could even get a lick in! They never knew what hit them.

    They managed to stumble into the doors of their awaiting vehicle. Once inside rubber was burned!

"Thank you." The lady showed gratitude.

She grabbed both of his hands then stared at him eye to eye for a moment.

"*Nama-Eyoni*." She uttered with a strong accent. Then slowly released his hands. This was certainly a new encounter for him.

"What does that mean?" He was curious.

"Holy man." She locked eyes on him again.

"Holy man? Me? Nawgh, wrong guy." Silky shrugged it off. "Definitely the wrong guy."

"*Ehenowe*." She was saying thus they say.

    She picked her bag up off the ground while maintaining seriousness. His troops were in awe. He was still surprised at his reflexes himself. Playing superhero wasn't his steelo, it was pure instincts. Before he could turn and walk off, she insisted, "I go with you."

"Something very different is happening here." He thought to himself.

Even his crew sensed the same. Notwithstanding, a new passenger was about to climb aboard.

"What's your name?" Silky asked.

"Kanaka." After answering she pointed at him.

"They call me Silky Black. Did you know those men?"

"No, I've never seen them before. They might follow me from café. I sing and make money."

The gold car began to move again. On and off small talk ensued, causing a few smiles and laughs. They made another pitstop in Joplin, Missouri. It was time to grab a bite to eat, so one of the bars on the river was chosen.

Kanaka immediately went to find the manager or owner. After speaking with the manager, she joined the others at the table. She told Silky what she would like once asked, then temporarily excused herself.

"I'll be right back."

Silky nodded in acknowledgement, anticipating a decent meal; they all were. A few funny looks surfaced, but they could care less.

They witnessed Kanaka stepping onto a small stage. After grabbing the microphone, she began singing. The native American woman sung three songs before leaving the stage. Most of the attendees clapped and cheered once she finished. The manager gave her the small funds agreed upon.

Afterwards, Kanaka gave the money to Silky Black. The whole crew was impressed, even Silky. While seated they overheard multiple conversations. One group were discussing the plane crash that killed six people in February that year. One couple was discussing how Route 66 was near its decommission.

A couple of others were still celebrating the state championship win from Joplin Memorial High School boys' basketball team. They went on to win the state championship the next year too. Once their stomachs and tank were filled it was time to move on.

In about 2 ½ hours they would enter Kansas City. If things went right a few nights of stay were planned. There was a mafia conflict going on at the time. Two bars were bombed earlier that year which led to more gang violence.

The Royals played well that year, and large concerts were being held in their stadium. Silky tried to find a spot that wasn't mafia related, so Kanaka could have a safe place to sing. Meanwhile, the streets weren't too safe either. There was a new serial killer on the loose, deemed the Kansas City Strangler, focusing on prostitutes.

He didn't get arrested and convicted until the new millennium surfaced with DNA evidence linking him to the murders. The mafia was trying to establish a red-light district in the River Quay area, with the introduction of prostitution and strip joints.

One of Silky's girls got clamped by the fuzz! Soon as he received word, he went to go get her. He had to pay a fine, plus she had to spend three days in jail. The city had declared a "War on Prostitution." Once she was released, he grabbed the girls then split town. They stayed a week; under the circumstances things still went fairly well.

The troops soon stomped the ground in Milwaukee, St. Louis, and Memphis. After three or four months on the road they were finally heading home.

The last stop was Dallas before ending their trip. The Dallas Cowboys would go on to win the Super Bowl that year; but that wasn't the sport the basketball star was concerned about. Silky headed towards the Cedar Springs area, known for prostitution and a lively nightlife.

He put his girls down, got Kanaka set up at a club, then rubbed elbows with a few players at the club. By this time, Silky's popularity had begun to grow nationwide. They stayed a few nights then headed home. Everybody was tired when they returned. Some of the places they went seemed worth returning to, others would just become distant memories.

It was time to take advantage of their hometown's amenities. Silky Black entered a club called The Blue Ice near the VA hospital and saw a couple of familiar faces. The next day, he decided to let his main girls take on more responsibility for the next week or two. He hadn't given up on basketball just yet, so some soul searching had to take place.

The traveler felt he had some unfinished business in Dallas, so he had Dana ride there with him. They entered an establishment on Harry Hines Boulevard. After thirty minutes or so they exited. While walking to the car, they were approached by a man in expensive clothes, that appeared to be suffering from lack of sleep.

"Dana come here!" The man yelled.

Silky and Dana turned towards the yelling man. Then Dana looked at Silky as to say that's him. They both stopped for a moment.

"She's with me, and if it's not about money she ain't going nowhere."

"I'm all about money so she needs to come with me."

"Go get in the car." Silky handed her the keys.

Dana did as she was told. She knew that this dude was crazy, so she was hoping everything went smoothly. She didn't want to get in the car but chose to be obedient. She wanted to be near her man.

"Man, are you going to release my hoe or what?"

"Dana's been with me for years, so how do you figure she belong to you?"

"She's always going to belong to me!"

"I understand you might be short on hoes, but don't come trying to gorilla me!"

As Silky was about to turn and walk away, the mad gorilla pimp pulled a gun out then fired! Two bullets entered Silky Black's legs! The gunman turned and walked away as his victim fell to the ground. Dana ran to his side, crying and screaming!

Someone inside the club called the ambulance, when it arrived Dana followed in Silky's car. Once at the hospital for a while an update was given.
The doctor said his tibia was shattered along with minor nerve damage. Thankfully, there were no life-threatening injuries.

"How bad is it doc? You know I play basketball, I'm about to go to the big leagues."

"I'm sorry Mr. Townsend; I don't think that will be happening."

Leon's head dropped! He felt a blow stronger than the gunshots. All his hopes and aspirations gone in an instant. A couple of tears fell from his face. The streets seemed to make his choice for him, or had he already chosen and was in denial?

He had to wear a cast and use crutches for a while. The news didn't sit well with him nor anyone that really cared. Eventually, his injuries would improve, but his potential basketball career was a thing of the past. The hard thinker felt there was no reason to hold back any longer.

For the next few years Silky Black went into overdrive. He had a hard time convincing his parents to move, but with time they finally gave in. He bought them a new house, cars, and all. Silky Black had revenue coming in from multiple cities. His game had expanded tremendously.

Cadillacs, Rolls Royces, and limos became normal tools of his. He kept upgrading his living situation too. As they would say in the future, he was ballin'!

# Chapter 10: The Second Half

It was now the eighties, and the seventies were history. Silky received a call from Shirley early one morning. He offered to let her live with him on several occasions, as much as she wanted to, she still declined. He answered while yawning.

"Hello."

"It's me Shirley. Did I wake you?"

"I'm ok. What's up?"

"I need you to go to the hospital with me."

"What's going on?"

"I want to go see my uncle."

He really didn't want to go, but said," Ok, I'll go with you."

Three hours later they arrived at Herman Hospital. Silky Black's walk was slightly different since being shot. Shirley knew Silky would be shocked once walking in the room.

When they stepped into the room Shirley spoke in a calm tone. "Hey Unc."

He spoke back, "Hey niece."

When Silky saw who her uncle was, he said, "Wait a minute. Nawgh….Mr. Wonderful….Man, how are you?"

"I'm hanging in there Mr. Silky Black."

The visitors took a seat, then focused on him.
Silky was still in disbelief. He looked back and forth at both of them, shaking his head.

"Why didn't somebody tell me what was what?"

"She begged me not to tell you. She has some other things to share with you too."

Shirley began to speak, "I never sold my body Leon. I was robbing tricks for you. I'm still a virgin."

"She loves you Silky."

Silky was wondering what was going on. All of this was coming to him at the same time. He still didn't know why Mr. Wonderful was in the hospital.

"I've been diagnosed with cancer youngblood. I'm cool though; it is what it is."

"I hate to hear that."

"Pray for me."

Silky Black was shocked, he never heard his mentor talk like that before. They stayed for about an hour or two before leaving. Shirley wanted to know what he was thinking, but Silky remained quiet for most of the ride. He dropped her off then headed home. When he walked through the door, Kanaka was sitting patiently waiting.

"I need to talk to you."

He could see that her bags were packed near the door. He went to sit near her.

"*Ehani Macha-Mahaiyu Nah-Hiwatama Vihnivo Napave.* Our Father, The Great Mystery, The Ruler of the sun, has been merciful to me. Happily, I go on my way in peace. *Tze-Ihutzittu Nimadzi Nai.* When I go my way carry healing. Thank you for everything."

She kissed him on the forehead then headed to the door. Unlike most, it saddened him a little to see her go. He walked her to the door.

Surprisingly, he said, "Bless you."

The door was softly closed behind her. Then he sat back down to gather his thoughts. He found joy in Ruthy having her own tailoring storefront and helping to make it possible. He weighed the good and bad in his life for a moment, realizing the lessons learned from the good, bad, and the ugly.

Still, he was engulfed in much sin; so much until spiritual blindness was still upon him.
His method of thinking and logic was far off from most. He could care less, he was surviving. Silky sat back recalling some of the recent happenings.

He jumped up, then poured a glass of wine; tired of thinking too much. The native Fifth Ward resident operated as usual, navigating through obstacles and pushing forward. The loss of his ability to move forward with basketball haunted him more than he displayed.

He chose not to talk about it, nor squander in what ifs. He had to keep playing the cards dealt.

While out in the mix Silky Black came across a familiar face. Seeing this person instantly enraged him, it was the soursop that shot him. He wanted to beat him unconscious but didn't know if he was strapped or not.

They were in the parking lot of a club in Southwest Houston. A few years had passed but it didn't matter. Silky Black approached his target, brandished his weapon, then fired! He had a cruel grimace as the bullets penetrated his foe's body.

Four bullets entered various places on his body. When he fell, Silky Black had to do some split-second thinking.

"Do I want to walk up on him to finish him, or just let the dice roll?"

He really didn't want to kill him, what he did was revenge enough, so he jumped in his car and drove off. Still, not knowing if he would survive or not.
A couple of days later, Silky received a call from Pink Paradise.

"I heard you popped that fool. He deserved it. Everybody knows how smooth you are Silky. He's a clown though, none of us respect him."

"I couldn't let him make it like that."

"I heard he's in bad shape. He's not stiff like he pretends. I wouldn't be surprised if he presses charges on you. I'm just giving you heads up man. Handle your business and lay low for a while."

"I appreciate it Pinky, stay cool."

They hung up. Silky Black got with his team, then prepped them on what to do if he got locked up. A week later, the word was out that an arrest warrant had been issued. Just as predicted, the scatterbrain told the authorities that Silky black shot him. He stayed in the hospital for a couple of months.

Silky Black decided to stay on the road for a while. He managed to evade the police for about six months. After posting bond he continued with his normal activities. On the day of his sentencing the courtroom was packed. Even a couple of his player partners showed up.

The judge wanted to give him twenty years, but since it was his first offense he was sentenced to ten years and a $5,000 fine. Some of Silky's girls started crying, while others contained their sorrow. Some of his family shed a few tears as well. Earl Jr. didn't show up, claiming he couldn't stand to see his baby brother get locked up. As they took Silky Black away in handcuffs, his people gave their support.

"We love you Silky Black!" His quad cheered.

"Stay strong my brother." Abdul encouraged.

"We love you son." His parents shared.

The words of encouragement kept coming from his supporters until he was out of sight. This was absolutely a new chapter for him. The question many had was, will his dynasty survive? Some even wondered if he would survive. They didn't feel he was weak; situations just occur.

It was 1985, the intake process took a month for Leon at TDC; confined with no tv nor other amenities.

The huge redneck guards constantly called the Black inmates niggers. They developed rank by whooping inmates. Once processed, Silky received a uniform with his TDC number and name printed on the shirt. He had gray and blue zip up pants with belt loops.

The following year these pants would become obsolete. Surprisingly, the food was plentiful. They were served steak, whole catfish, whole fruit, nuts, and ice cream. They had free iron weights which would change in years to come, because the inmates were getting too strong, which caused a threat to the guards.

Women had just recently started becoming correctional officers. Food at commissary was cheaper than the regular store, until the mid-nineties. Money and stamps passed easily which gave Silky easy action at making money on the inside too. He was trying to learn as much as possible, as quickly as possible.

He was told that it was easy to get furloughed with a limit of seven days if needed. Silky Black's popularity was evident in prison as well.

He had already become an underground legend. Some of the other inmates were taking turns trying to get game from him. Even some of the guards wanted info to improve their relationships.

It didn't take long for Leon to get settled in. He was determined to make the best out of it. Letters and money kept coming in. One day a new inmate came in that was supposed to be separated but wasn't for some reason. The openly gay inmates were separated but easy to get to for the lurkers.

He introduced himself to the inmates as Bubbles. He was slim and about 5'8. Bubbles tried to act manly around the guards so he could stay in general population. One guy decided to be nosy.

"Why do they call you Bubbles?"

"Catch me when the lights go out and I'll show you."

The guy punched Bubbles in the face. Bubbles took a couple of steps back to gain focus, then charged him while wildly windmilling! Then he posted up like a man and started punching like an amateur boxer!

The guy started fighting back but suddenly hit the floor. That wasn't the last time they witnessed Bubbles handling business either. Eventually, the administration corrected their error by placing Bubbles with the guys wearing lipstick made from cool offs.

Shirley and Dana went to visit one day as normal, but this visit was different. Silky noticed the variation in their demeanor. He didn't like it either.

"What's going on?"

He sensed hesitation. "Just spit it out."

Shirley softly spoke, "My uncle passed away Leon."

Leon dropped his head, being speechless for a moment. He didn't want to believe it and didn't know what to say. He grabbed his head, trying to hold back tears, taking deep breaths. They were all silent for a minute, giving him time to try and process it.

Dana said, "He had a nice service, plenty of people showed up and gave their support to the family."

"He had a lot of love for you." Shirley added.

Silky finally spoke, "I hope nobody else I'm close to croaks while I'm in here."

They discussed some business issues before leaving. The income gradually began to decrease in his absence, which was expected anyway. Things were rougher for some than others, especially those with lengthy sentences. Some would rather die than see another day in prison.

Many more prisons were being built in Texas, they were filling up fast too. Especially with crack cocaine on the scene now. Silky kept himself busy with various activities, including learning trades, cautiously playing basketball, reading books, and so on. He met a man one day that had two life sentences named Shacar, while in the prison library.

Shacar had an impressive physique and chose to exercise his mind as much as his body. Both men were respected; however, Shacar had a sense of seniority because of his age, sentence, and time served. Not to mention the track record of wins in combat.

Shacar told Silky, "I see you're pretty popular in and out of here. Once you're here long enough people will forget about you. I learned that from experience."

Silky responded, "Well, I guess as long as I don't forget about myself, I'll be alright."

"Can I ask you something Silky Black?"

"Sure."

"If it's not too personal, where do you stand with your faith?"

"That's a good question. I believe in GOD. I don't go to church or a mosque, or anything like that.
My old lady went to church sometimes; she took me before when I was a kid."

"Young brother, I'm never getting out of here.
I encourage you to allow me to share some things with you. Hopefully, you will share it with others.
We all have a purpose, and I'm trying to fulfill mine."

Silky felt the seriousness of his tone, demeanor, and spirit. Leon was all ears.

This was just the first of the many conversations they would have concerning their faith. Silky began to look forward to these conversations, which compelled him to research and study for himself. Time brought change, change indeed.

Shirley entered the visitation room. Silky could always tell when something was wrong. After greeting her he said, "Ok Shirley lay it on me."

"Dana and two other girls are gone. They started smoking rocks." She was shaking her head while speaking.

"What?" Silky wanted to punch the wall but restrained himself.

Shirley continued, "The out-of-town money isn't coming in like it's supposed to. Some of the girls have been getting clipped, and no new ones are coming in."

"Bring all the girls in from every city, we have to run a tight ship from here on out."

"Yes, Silky Black." Shirley accepted her instructions.

Silky's empire was crumbling while behind bars, he strived to hold things together. After three years things changed drastically. One day he was called to the chaplain's office, which was always a sign of bad news. Once seated, the chaplain gave him the sad news.

"Mr. Leon Townsend, with sympathy and prayers I hate to inform you that your father has passed away."

The news felt like a punch to the gut. Leon cried and sobbed while grabbing his chest. After partially regaining composure he returned to his cell. Now it was time to request a furlough.
Mr. Townsend was killed by a drunk driver, leaving his family devastated.

As hoped for the furlough was granted. The Fifth Ward celebrity was allowed to mourn with his family. As much as he wanted to stay around them, the constant crying began to bother him. Plus, he was on borrowed time that had to be taken advantage of. He felt as if he was losing from every angle.

Silky knew he had to make his presence count, so he did as much as possible. Keeping his name alive in the streets was key to maintaining everything. Crack cocaine soon became the main competition for all the players. The smokers started off freebasing with glass pipes, then graduated to the metal straight shooters.

It was bad enough when the girls were on smack, now another drug hampered progress. Silky's crew had been drug free for the most part until now. He didn't like what he was seeing around him, but what was he going to do?

The bars enclosed him again, with many knuckleheads and a couple of friends. He couldn't wait to be free again but would have to. One day while watching the news, Silky couldn't believe his eyes as he helplessly watched his house burn! To make matters worse someone was being rolled out on a stretcher.

He couldn't see who it was either. Word came to him that crackheads had broken into Ruthy's store. Earline contracted an STD after being raped by an ex-boyfriend, Earl Jr. turned into a junkie, Mrs. Wilma went into a deep depression after losing Earl Sr., but Eugene was doing good for himself.

In 1990, the revolving door policy was introduced to TDC because of overcrowding, which almost guaranteed parole. Some people were released two or three times in one year. After five years Silky Black was released on parole.

He wasn't done yet; rebuilding was imperative to him. He went to Atlanta one deep, planning not to return the same. Silky still had tools even though he wanted to upgrade. He sold some of his prize possessions while incarcerated; still holding a torch to most.

He had a plan to implement. Upon finding what he considered the perfect motel; he went to work. He found a desperate owner on the verge of losing their property, then convinced them to collaborate with him.

He spruced the place up some, then set girls in place, basically starting from the ground up again. After things began to prosper he duplicated the same formula in two other cities. Silky even painted and did some manual labor himself, things learned in prison. Before long he looked like the old Silky Black.

He was invited to a Player's Ball in Chicago, so he attended. Like most pimps, he wanted to be recognized for his game. Players from all over the country were there. The excitement was building enormously as the pimp of the year was about to be announced.

Strangely enough, Silky Black, who could have easily been crowned, decided to just walk away.
He went to the airport not caring whether he had been awarded or not. It was at that very moment when he could have reached the pinnacle of his street sport, that he decided to give it all up.

It was time to regain focus; he stared in the mirror reminiscing long enough. There was a congregation full of people waiting to hear him speak.

Kanaka had tracked him down and gave him a nice amount of land in Oklahoma that she inherited from her family. After feeling that he was called to the ministry, Leon decided to build a church in Tulsa on the gifted property.

He began to speak, "Wake up Israel! We are the dry bones that can live. You must understand who you are, and whose you are. We've been lied to, for too long! Let the heathen have their pagan holidays. Cleave to what is holy and abandon the traditions of man.

King Solomon said to search for wisdom like a hidden treasure. That means we must dig for the truth. Stop accepting everything that's presented to you. We have been taught to embrace many things we need to let go. Open your mind and your heart!

Pray, fast, seek answers. The Most High is not being honored in many things we do. Fulfill your purpose while you still can. The enemy wants to keep you distracted while your life is expiring.
There's power in your praise! Power in your prayers!

He continued to preach while his wife and their daughter sat in the front row. The many conversations with Shacar played an important role, along with Kanaka and many others. His family was super proud of him. Some of them even moved to Tulsa to be with him.

That day, Mrs. Wilma was sitting next to Shirley and Peaches, his wife and daughter.

Made in the USA
Coppell, TX
10 February 2026